Through a Clouded Mirror

ALSO BY MIYA T. BECK

The Pearl Hunter

MIYA T. BECK

Through a Clouded Mirror

BALZER + BRAY
An Imprint of HarperCollinsPublishers

Balzer + Bray is an imprint of HarperCollins Publishers.

Through a Clouded Mirror
Copyright © 2024 by Miya T. Beck
All rights reserved. Printed in the United States of America.
No part of this book may be used or reproduced in any manner
whatsoever without written permission except in the case of
brief quotations embodied in critical articles and reviews. For
information address HarperCollins Children's Books, a division of
HarperCollins Publishers, 195 Broadway, New York, NY 10007.
www.harpercollinschildrens.com

Library of Congress Control Number: 2023944077
ISBN 978-0-06-323824-4

Typography by Molly Fehr
24 25 26 27 28 LBC 5 4 3 2 1
First Edition

For Talia, Emma, Ellie, Zac, and Trevor,
May you always believe in as many as six
impossible things before breakfast.

"BUT I SUPPOSE THIS DREAM OF MINE
IS RATHER ABSURD."

—Sei Shōnagon, *The Pillow Book*

1

Hateful Things

Yuki Snow was down to her last envelope. She'd started with twenty on moving day, on that August afternoon when she had left the only home she'd ever known in the San Fernando Valley for the new house in Santa Dolores. As the truck pulled away with all their belongings, her mother had handed Yuki and her best friend, Julio, gift bags containing prestamped, pre-addressed envelopes and special stationery—with a lion stalking across the top for Yuki, and a tiger stretching in the lower right corner for Julio. Next-door neighbors who shared the same birthday, Yuki and Julio loved to send low-tech messages to each other. With flashlights using Morse code. Over staticky CB radios. Through notes written in invisible ink. In that spirit, her mother had come up with this parting gift. Then Yuki and Julio had said their goodbyes by bumping fists and fluttering their hands, a move they'd been doing for as long as she could remember.

But now, one month later, sitting in English class with twelve minutes left in the period, Yuki was keenly aware of how lopsided their friendship had become. She was writing her twentieth letter to Julio, while Julio had sent her only two. One had contained a sketch of a video game character that he'd created. The other had been a printout of a touch-typing exercise from computer class. He had mistyped a bunch of words and thought she would get a good laugh: *We are such stuff as llamas are made of, and our piddly life is round with sheep. Sure, I am vexxed! Bear with my weak knees. My brain is troubled!* In pen, Julio had signed off as "The Bard of Typing" and added a PS: *The next columnist for the Buena Vista Middle School newspaper—ha ha.*

He found this hilarious because she was the writer, the one whose column, "The Snowdown," had been a must-read in every edition of the student newspaper, and the one who at age nine had dazzled her much-older competitors in the Cal State University Wonderland Slam. The slam had taken place two months before her father died from a blood clot following a routine surgery. A professor who taught philosophy classes based on *Alice's Adventures in Wonderland* and *Through the Looking-Glass*, her father had cofounded the annual poetry event for local high school students, and Yuki had been his helper. The contestants had ten minutes to write poems based on prompts from the Alice books, which they then read aloud, with half moving on to the next round until only two remained. On a whim, Yuki had done

2

the first prompt on the frumious Bandersnatch, which the judges loved so much that she suddenly went from helping at the contest to being *in* the contest. Six rounds later, Yuki squared off in the final against a high school junior named Ferny Bloom. Their challenge had been to write a poem about why a raven was like a writing desk. Yuki had written:

> *Becawse the wingspan of a bird in*
> *flight looks like a tabletop*
> *Becawse a drawer can be a nest and hold an unkindness*
> *Becawse Edgar Allan Poe sat down*
> *at one and wrote*
> *Nevermore*

Her father had glowed with pride as Yuki read her final poem onstage. Afterward, he had said, "That was fabulous, Monster!" which was an inside Alice joke that they shared. That had been the best day of Yuki's life, the day she started to believe she was going to be a great writer. But nobody at Juana Maria Middle School in Santa Dolores knew about the Wonderland Slam or "The Snowdown." Would her fellow eighth graders even notice if her desk dropped down into a rabbit hole or was carried off by a tornado? She guessed not.

Yuki chewed on her pen cap and peeked up the row at Ms. Ghosh, who had a helmet of gray hair and kept an egg timer on her desk. If Yuki had still been at her old middle school in the Valley, she would've been writing poetry based on

3

Emily Dickinson—using lots of—short lines—and dashes—like this—and working on her trademark "Top Five" list for her next column. But Juana Maria Middle School didn't have a newspaper, and Ms. Ghosh took all the poetry out of language by making them diagram sentences. Yuki had already finished the worksheet, and apparently so had all the kids around her, since they were all on their phones.

Yuki didn't have a phone yet, which was a source of great embarrassment. Not that she had anyone to text with anyway. She hadn't made a single friend since moving to Santa Dolores. When her mother asked who she wanted to invite to her birthday party, it took every ounce of her self-control to say calmly, "No one. Just the usual with Julio." Every year, Yuki and Julio had a special dinner of tempura and tamales. Everyone believed Yuki and Julio when they said they were cousins, because they both had thick dark brown hair and olive skin that tanned easily in the sun.

On a piece of notebook paper, Yuki wrote:

Hey Julio (a.k.a. Don't Call Me Julie-o),
Ten days until our birthday! I can't wait to see you and the old neighborhood! Santa Dolores is so snore-endous, I might as well be in Kansas with Toto. At least then I'd have a dog.
Today's list is Top 5 Reasons Why Juana Maria Middle School Should Get Canceled.

4

After writing down the numbers one through five, she frowned at the page. Her father used to tell her that the best way to get people's attention was to make them laugh. But nothing about her new life in Santa Dolores was funny. After remarrying last spring, her mother said she and Doug wanted a fresh start in a new home. Hana—who Yuki started calling by her first name on the day they moved—said houses cost less where Doug lived, forty-five miles up the coast. So that's where they had looked. Hana had supplied a steady stream of reasons why this was a good idea. Didn't Yuki want to live by the beach? Wouldn't Yuki like to breathe the fresh sea air? Wouldn't it be wonderful to drive to the grocery store without any traffic? In response, Yuki had written a list, something she used to do with her father.

1. *It would not be fun to live by the beach*
because sand gets everywhere, including in
the pages of whatever book I'm reading.
2. *The ocean has a fishy smell.*
3. *Smog is the original Instagram filter and creates*
amazing sunsets (not that I would know firsthand,
since I'm the only eighth grader without a phone).
4. *Traffic gives me more time to sing along to the radio.*
5. *Julio is my BFF and he lives in the Valley.*

Her father had always respected her reasons. Her mother, not so much. Over Yuki's objections, Hana and Doug had bought a house in Santa Dolores. And even though Yuki didn't like the beach, she'd been deeply disappointed to discover that they were not moving into a cute oceanside bungalow with a sign on the porch that read "This way for mermaids." No, the new house was four miles inland, amid dry foothills and citrus orchards.

With five minutes left before class ended, her reasons for canceling Juana Maria Middle School finally spilled onto the page.

1. Remember Island of the Blue Dolphins? *The school is named for the woman who inspired the book, which would be cool except Juana Maria is the name the mansplaining priests gave her after they took her off the island.*
2. All the walkways are dotted with wads of old gum, which is gross.
3. The school is across the street from a farm, so it smells like manure with a hint of stinky gym socks.
4. You are invisible unless you live in a fancy house up on the foothills and hang out at the Ondulando Club.
5. Do I really need any more reasons?
Your friend,
Yuki (a.k.a. Don't Call Me Yucky)

As Yuki tucked her letter into the envelope, Ms. Ghosh told them to pass up their papers.

"For homework, you'll be interviewing a senior, could be a grandparent or another relative, about a memory that's important to them," Ms. Ghosh said. "You could write about an event in their lives, or a keepsake that has a memory attached. This is not a biography that starts with them being born. The idea is to focus on the specific memory. Your papers are due Monday."

Yuki's hand shot up in the air.

"Yes, Yuki," Ms. Ghosh said without enthusiasm.

Ever since Yuki had asked Ms. Ghosh why she didn't use a rubric for grading papers, her English teacher had seemed annoyed with her. Yuki had received a 97 on her first essay and a rubric would have shown her why she'd lost three points. The teachers at her old middle school always used a rubric, she explained, to which Ms. Ghosh had said, "This is not your old school."

"What if you don't have any relatives who are seniors?" Yuki asked.

"How about a neighbor, then," Ms. Ghosh suggested.

"But I just moved here," Yuki said, anxiety making her words come out fast and high. She was going to fail an assignment because she was the new kid. That wasn't fair.

"Well, what a great way to meet new people," Ms. Ghosh said.

The bell rang. As Yuki leaned over to zip up her backpack, a hand covered in black doodles swiped the envelope from her desk. "Wow, you wrote an actual letter. That's so retro."

Yuki looked up to find two girls inspecting the envelope. Zoe wore Doc Martens with the shoelaces untied and had inked geometric patterns all the way up both arms. She looked like the kind of kid who would call Yuki a nerd and then ask to cheat off her paper. Ava was a pretty blonde who hung out at the popular kids' picnic table. She looked like the type who would smile to Yuki's face and then call her a nerd behind her back. That's what used to happen at her old school, but it hadn't mattered so much, since she had Julio.

Ava peered over Zoe's shoulder. "Julio Garcia-Jones," she said. "He sounds cute."

"Can I have my letter back?" Yuki said, standing up and holding out her hand.

Ava grabbed the envelope from Zoe. "Is it a love letter? Is Julio your boyfriend?"

Zoe snatched it back. "Ooh, do you guys say 'I love you' to each other?"

"Give it back!" Yuki shrieked. She lunged for the envelope, grabbed one end, and accidentally ripped it in two. Zoe's eyes went wide with shock. The portion in her hand fluttered to the floor.

"What is going on here?" Ms. Ghosh said, glaring at them from her desk.

Yuki scooped up the other half of the letter from the floor and marched out of the room. There was an angry buzz in her ears, a swarm of wasps in her head.

"I'm sorry," she heard Zoe say. "I was just messing around. I wasn't going to read it."

Ava giggled. "Oh my God, Zoe. I'm so telling Aunt Margie on you."

Now it made sense. Tweedledee and Tweedledum were cousins. Why else would a popular girl and a Goth girl hang out together? Yuki walked faster along the gum-speckled hallway. She hated this place. This was all her mother's fault. Clutching the ripped letter in her hand, she hurried out to the bike racks and unlocked her baby blue beach cruiser. The bike had been a gift from Doug. Besides telling dorky jokes, he was always buying her gifts and trying to get her to like him—which, out of loyalty to her father, she never would.

Yuki biked up a hill with houses on one side and a citrus orchard on the other. She missed the jacarandas on her old street, which exploded with purple flowers every June. Then the blossoms fell and turned the asphalt lavender for a few magical weeks. Though she wasn't in the mood to go home, she didn't know where else to go. As Yuki glided toward the tan house with the drought-resistant yard, the lowered red flag on the mailbox taunted her. She opened the metal door and sighed. No letter from Julio, only a coupon pack and a knitting catalog called Darned If You Do.

After parking her bike in the garage, Yuki entered the silent house. Back in the Valley, she had never minded being home alone, because she always had a book or an album from her father's extensive collection to get lost in. In the new house, most of his belongings were still in boxes in the garage. Now that she no longer lived in the Valley, Yuki missed her father even more. She remembered his exuberance when he exclaimed, "'Twas brillig!" even if it wasn't four o'clock, and "I am Oz, the great and terrible. Why do you seek me?" to students who came to his office hours. She remembered his trimmed beard and his sparkly brown eyes magnified by his glasses. But his face overall was no longer sharp in her mind, and sometimes she studied her parents' wedding photo to burn the picture into her memory. Her father had been barefoot in the photo, and the flower on his lapel had tilted sideways.

If only Yuki were turning eighteen on her birthday, she could leave Santa Dolores forever. She'd move back to the Valley and go to Cal State, where her dad used to teach. She'd write for the campus literary journal and her professors would say how bright and funny she was, just like her father. After graduation, she would write a novel in verse, something important like *Brown Girl Dreaming*, and then she would be famous. Creative instead of weird. Smart instead of a nerd. All the kids who had teased her would wish they had been nicer.

After reuniting the two halves of her letter with tape, Yuki searched her mother's desk for a fresh envelope and a stamp. But the stamp pack was empty. Maybe she could type her letter into an email instead, using her school account. Going down the hall to her bedroom, she woke up her desktop computer. Clicking on the envelope icon, she started typing Julio's email address, pausing when she reached the @ symbol. Did he check his school email? Probably not. He messaged with Troy and other gamer friends on a site called LVLup.

The computer was strictly for homework. But since Yuki was a rule follower, her mother probably hadn't bothered to set up parental controls. Opening a new tab, Yuki searched for LVLup and clicked on the sign-up form. When she reached a question about whether she was over thirteen, she wavered. Clearly Julio had lied. As she clicked the "yes" box and hit "submit," Yuki imagined a siren wailing and a fleet of internet security police showing up at the front door. But setting up a secret online account turned out to be a shockingly quiet and easy thing to do.

She chose the screen name CL4ever, for the Cowardly Lion. Then she searched for Tig1010. "Lions and tigers and bears" had been their favorite part of *The Wizard of* Oz in kindergarten, back when they used to watch the movie every weekend, running a play tunnel between their blanket fort and the TV, which they pretended was a portal to Oz.

Lions and tigers and bears, she DMed. Three dots appeared.

Tig1010: Oh my! Yuki??? I can't believe you're here!

CL4ever: Surprise! I wrote you a letter but then realized I'm out of stamps.

Tig1010: Sorry I haven't written you back. I owe you a million letters by now.

Tig1010: The most hilarious thing happened in computer class today. I got busted by Mr. Wilson for passing a note to Suzie. But since I wrote, "Hey, you quick brown fox," and Suzie wrote back, "Hey, you lazy dog," Mr. W said he'd give us extra credit for using a typing exercise.

Yuki felt a twinge of envy. Mr. Wilson was the most popular teacher in eighth grade. During the touch-typing unit, he played classical music, waved a baton, and told them which key to hit in time to the beat. If you happened to pass by, you'd hear him calling out, "A-A-A, F, G-G-G, D," while fifty students tapped their keyboards in unison.

CL4ever: I miss all the good stuff. Why were you flirting with Stuck-up Suzie?

Tig1010: Be nice.

CL4ever: Why? She's never been nice to me.

Besides acting like she was better than everyone, Suzie was also a thief. In third grade, Yuki had caught her stealing two Pokémon cards from another kid. Yet somehow Suzie had remained as popular as ever.

Tig1010: You don't like it when kids make fun of you for being smart.

CL4ever: I am smart. And Suzie is stuck up. Why are you defending her?

His three reply dots bubbled and then vanished. Was he not going to answer? Where had he gone? The suspense was too much. Waiting for an instant message was even more painful than checking the mailbox. At least with snail mail, you knew you had to wait another twenty-four hours for the next delivery.

CL4ever: Are you still there?

No response. Not even the three reply dots.

"Yuki, what is this?"

Yuki jumped in her seat. In a panic, she clicked the red dot instead of the yellow dot, closing the browser. Of course, the one time she broke the rules, Hana had come home early.

2

Mysterious Things

Yuki spun around in her chair to find her mother standing in the doorway with her disapproving origami crane face, all sharp points and angles. Hana was still dressed for work, in a black pantsuit with her hair in a sleek bun. Even though her mother had been born in Tokyo, she had split time between Japan and the US as a kid and spoke flawless English, so perfect that she overemphasized each sound and made each syllable distinct. When people said "be-*cuz*" instead of "be-*caws*," her mother always shuddered a bit.

"I was checking my math test grade on StudentStats," Yuki said, startled that the lie rolled off her tongue just as easily as starting up a secret online account.

"What?" Hana said, confused. "Oh, no, I was asking why this is inside my yarn basket in the den?" She held up a Frisbee-size mirror still partially covered in bubble wrap.

"I've never seen that before," Yuki said.

"It has your name on it," Hana said, showing her a yellow sticky note.

"What are you talking about?" Yuki marched over to take a closer look. The sticky note had two symbols, one that looked like a fish and the other that looked like a tree branch.

"That's your name in Japanese," Hana said.

Footsteps rushed up the staircase. "That's supposed to be a surprise," Doug called out, his glasses fogging and his gray-brown hair hanging limply over his forehead. "It's a birthday present for Yuki."

Hana's thin, penciled eyebrows formed two peaks. "Why would you buy her a mirror? And why would you leave it in my yarn basket?"

"Because you never knit and Yuki would never look there," Doug said. "It's a special mirror. Look, I'll show you. Yuki, where's your flashlight?"

Doug crossed her room and leaned the mirror against the computer monitor on her desk. Yuki sighed with exasperation as she opened the drawer in her nightstand and handed him one of the twelve flashlights he had bought and stashed all over the house in case of an emergency. She didn't want Hana and Doug in her room. But the fastest way to get them out was to cooperate.

Doug turned on the flashlight and aimed the beam at the mirror.

"It's not quite dark enough in here," he said, pointing to

15

the opposite wall. "Can you see the lion?"

Yuki squinted at the shimmering light on the wall. She could just make out a curly mane. "Barely," she said.

"It's the *komainu*," her mother said. "Remember the statues we saw in Japan?"

"Oh yeah," Yuki said. The *komainu* was more of a cross between a lion and a dog, and they guarded the temples and shrines.

"They sell these magic mirrors at a Japanese emporium downtown," Doug said, turning off the flashlight and setting it on the desk. "Since you have a lot of stuff with lions on it, I thought you might get a kick out of this."

"There's a Japanese emporium downtown?" Hana asked.

"There is," Doug said. "I was looking for a gift for our anniversary."

"Your anniversary isn't until May," Yuki said.

Hana beamed. "Tonight is the anniversary of our first date. We have theater tickets."

That's why they'd come home early. Doug danced her mother around in a circle. They laughed, making googly eyes at each other. Ugh. Yuki thought she might be sick.

"Could you guys do that somewhere else?" Yuki said. "I have homework."

"I guess you might as well keep the mirror now that you've seen it," Doug said, sticking his hands in his pockets and shrugging his shoulders. "Happy birthday."

"Thanks," she said, telegraphing her disdain for him in one flat syllable.

"Watch the sass," her mother warned.

Yuki shrugged, though inside she squirmed. She knew she was being mean. After they left, she checked LVLup again. Julio had not responded, and the little blue dot was no longer by his avatar. She refreshed their chat over and over. In seventh grade, Yuki and Julio had both been nauseated by all the drama around who was going out with who, and they'd made fun of the awkward slow dancing at the middle school spring fling. Julio only cared about gaming and drawing. He couldn't possibly have a crush on Suzie. Could he?

Before they left for the theater, Hana made an early dinner. Yuki grimaced at the plate of spaghetti with hot dog slices mixed into the sauce. When her mother tried to cook like an American, she sometimes combined odd things, like hamburger patties with rice on the side, or plain omelets sweetened with sugar and drizzled in soy sauce. Doug cut his noodles in a crisscross pattern while Hana twirled the spaghetti around her fork into a beehive capped by a slice of hot dog.

"How was school today?" Hana asked, her hair loose and wavy now.

"The usual," Yuki said, shoving the hot dog slices to the side of her plate.

"My coworker's niece goes to your school," Hana said. "Isabella. Do you know her?"

"There are, like, five Isabellas in my grade," Yuki said. "They all belong to the Ondulando Club, and they use their one collective brain cell to make videos of themselves tanning

17

by the pool, which is the online equivalent of watching paint dry. Not that I would know, since I don't have a phone."

The origami crane face returned. "I'm just trying to help, Yuki," Hana said. "This Isabella sounds like a nice girl."

"Well, Hana, you want to help? Let's move back to the Valley," Yuki said.

The lines around her mother's mouth deepened with annoyance.

"You know, I had moved four times by your age," Hana said. "To make new friends, you have to be open to new people and new experiences."

"I don't want new friends," Yuki said. "I already have a best friend."

"Moving is not the end of the world," Hana said. "It's what you make of it."

"It's not the end of the world for *you*," Yuki said. "You aren't a Valley diehard like Dad and me." Her father had loved the Valley, which was quirky and unhip compared to the Westside. He always said he would rather teach the first-generation college students at Cal State than the superstars fighting for spots at UCLA.

Hana muttered under her breath in Japanese. They ate in silence for several long minutes until Doug leaned over and stabbed a piece of hot dog on Yuki's plate with his fork.

"You're not eating your hot dog," he said. "That's the best part."

"Only if you like gristle and little bony bits," Yuki said. "Hot dogs aren't good for you."

"When you start making dinner, then you can complain about my cooking," Hana said.

Yuki glared at her mother. Mild alarm entered Doug's eyes.

"Hey, I've got a new one for you, Yuki," he said with forced cheer. "A black hole walks into a bar. The bartender says, 'Why so glum?' And the black hole says, 'It's a dark matter.'"

Yuki stifled a laugh. When Doug first started dating Hana, he had vowed to make Yuki laugh at one of his silly jokes, which meant she had no choice but to keep a straight face. She cupped her hand around her ear. "That was the galaxy groaning," she said.

Doug gave her a goofy grin. "Oh, come on," he said. "It's a little bit funny."

"No, it's not," she said. "Your jokes are where funny goes to die."

Even as the words came out of her mouth, Yuki knew she had gone too far. Hana set down her fork with a clatter. "Okay, that's it," her mother said. "I've had enough of your attitude. Go to your room."

"Gladly," Yuki huffed.

From her bed, Yuki shined the flashlight into the mirror. She wished she could climb onto the back of the lion and run away, either to the past with her father or to the future when she'd be old enough to live on her own and return to the Valley. *Julio should be the one trying to cheer me up with lion gifts, not Doug,* she thought. She had planned to get Julio a T-shirt that read "I paused my game for you" for his birthday. But this Suzie thing had created a sense of urgency. Yuki needed to find the perfect gift, something that would remind him that she had always been his best friend.

In the morning before school, Yuki stashed all the allowance she had saved, twenty-nine dollars, in her backpack. Then she went to the kitchen, where Doug was at the counter pouring a cup of coffee.

"Yuki, I've got a new one for you," Doug said. "A chicken and an egg are at the bar waiting to order and the bartender says, 'Which one of you was first?'"

Yuki pressed her lips together, determined not to laugh. "Sorry, try again later," she said.

"I will," he said, looking a bit too pleased.

"Hey, I was wondering about the mirror," Yuki said. "What other designs did the shop have besides the lion?"

"Oh, there was a flower and a bird—a whole bunch," Doug said.

"Anything else?" she asked.

"I think there was a cat." Doug said. "Why? Do you want to exchange yours for a different one?"

She had hoped Doug would say "tiger," because that's what she wanted to get for Julio. When they were little, his favorite book had been a pop-up that came with a flashlight. By beaming the flashlight behind the cutouts, he could cast shadow pictures on the wall. She was absolutely certain Julio would love that the Japanese mirror held a secret unlocked by a flashlight.

"No, I like the lion," Yuki said. "I was just curious."

At school as she made her way to her first class, nobody said hi to her and she didn't say hi to anyone. Unlike her old school, Juana Maria Middle School was mostly white and wealthy. The kids of color were nearly all Latinx, and there didn't seem to be much mixing between the two groups. Yuki didn't know if the other students ignored her because she was part Asian and therefore didn't fit in, or because she was a nerd and therefore not cool, or because her family didn't belong to the Ondulando Club. Or maybe it was the overlap of all three in her personal Venn diagram.

In social studies class, the teacher put her in a group with Ava to write a skit on the Egyptian gods. As Yuki mulled giving Ava the cold shoulder over the letter incident, the other boy assigned to their group put his head down on his desk to take a nap, which meant he would be no help at all.

"What about a game show where Anubis weighs the hearts of the dead," Yuki suggested, her desire for an A overriding her hurt feelings. "We could have a panel of gods and goddesses guessing whether the heart will weigh more or less than the feather of truth on the scale."

"I get to be Cleopatra," Ava said as she cocked her head and took a selfie with her phone.

"Cleopatra was a ruler, not a goddess," Yuki pointed out.

"Then I want to be Venus," Ava said.

"Venus is a Roman goddess, not Egyptian," Yuki said. "The Egyptian goddess of love is Hathor."

For the rest of the period, Yuki worked on the skit by

21

herself. She decided her small revenge would be not telling Ava that Hathor had the head of a cow.

At lunch, rather than sit alone in the courtyard, Yuki went to the library and did homework. When school was over, she rode downtown to Main Street, where she passed a frilly boutique next to a cavernous Goodwill next to a gleaming microbrewery next to a divey bar. If not for the paw-waving cats in the window, Yuki might have missed the faded Rising Sun Emporium sign. How had Doug found this place? He must have made a wrong turn on his way to the khakis store.

A bell chimed overhead as she entered the shop, which was filled with folding screens, calligraphy scrolls, vases, and large serving dishes. Along a shelf at eye level, more waving cats in different sizes batted their paws. She smiled and picked up one about the size of a saltshaker.

"No touching!" a sharp voice said.

She was so startled that she almost dropped the cat. "Sorry," Yuki called out.

The shopkeeper had short tufts of graying hair, wide-set eyes each resting on a double pouch of eyelid skin, and the dour mouth of a startled ostrich. Her white turtleneck had glittery gold streaks like a marbled bank building, and she wore large pearl-studded earrings that looked more like brooches. Yuki guessed the woman was in her sixties.

"You are looking for something?" the shopkeeper said gruffly.

"I heard you sell magic mirrors here," Yuki said.

The woman stood up and waved her toward the counter. Clicking on a flashlight, she angled the beam at two rows of dish-size mirrors on the wall. "These are called *makkyo* in Japanese. Bird, tree, cat, flower," she said, moving the beam left to right, pausing on each one. "Many kinds. Which do you like?"

"Do you have a tiger?" Yuki asked.

The beam came to rest on a mirror in the bottom row. "This one," she said.

Yuki admired the image of the tiger on the wall, which had a curlicue tail and raised front paws, as if in motion. "How much is it?"

"Forty-five dollars," the shopkeeper said. "Plus tax."

Yuki's shoulders slumped beneath her backpack. "I don't have enough money," she said. "I'll have to come back."

"Okay, you come back," the woman said, turning off the flashlight and sitting down again. She picked up a metal plate and a rag from the counter. From the back, the plate looked like an oversize ancient coin.

Yuki didn't move. Her eyes burned. A weary feeling washed over her. All she wanted to do was get Julio a memorable gift.

The shopkeeper frowned. "Is there something else?"

"No." Yuki lowered her eyes. "I just had a bad day. A bad two days. Actually, a bad month. I moved here over the summer and the kids at my school aren't very nice."

The woman stopped rubbing the dish. "I understand," she

said. "A new place can be hard."

Yuki's gaze fell on the woman's business card in a wood box on the counter. *Momo Fujita*, it read. She knew that *momo* meant "peach" in Japanese.

"My mom is from Japan," Yuki said. "From Tokyo."

Momo resumed her polishing. "I am from Osaka. But I have lived in Santa Dolores for many years."

"We went to Japan to visit my grandmother once and traveled all around," Yuki said. "We had pancakes in Osaka with seafood and vegetables in them. We cooked them at our table."

Momo perked up. "*Okonomiyaki*," she said. "Did you like this? It is very different from pancakes at IHOP."

"I did," Yuki said. "I also liked the drum cakes. *Taiko-*something."

"Ah, yes," Momo said. "*Taiko manju*. Sometimes I drive to Little Tokyo to find them."

Momo walked over to the wall, stretched on her tiptoes in her glittery gold sneakers, and took down the tiger mirror. "Since you like this one, I will hold it for you," she said.

"Thanks," Yuki said, looking at the tiger etched on the back. "How does the mirror cast the image on the wall?"

Momo pointed to the tiger. "Where the mirror maker etches the design on the back, that changes the thickness of the metal when it is forged," she said. "This creates the pattern when you shine the light into it."

Yuki set down her backpack and took out a notebook and a pen. Flipping to the first clean page, she wrote *makyo*,

24

followed by the description Momo had given her of how the mirror was made.

Momo squinted. "*Makkyo* has two *k*. Double *k*. Why do you write this down?"

"I write everything down," Yuki said. "It's my thing."

Momo waved her French-manicured nails over the notebook. "What will you do with this?"

Yuki hugged the notebook to her chest. "I don't know. Maybe nothing. I like to make lists and rank things. Like I could put your store on a list of the only cool places in Santa Dolores. I would just have to find some more first." *Which could take a while*, she thought.

"Oh, I see," Momo said, nodding sagely. "If you like lists and you like Japan, then you must read *The Pillow Book*. Do you know Sei Shōnagon?"

When Yuki shook her head, Momo took one of her business cards from the box on the counter and printed *Sei Shōnagon* in block letters on the back. "She was a lady in the imperial court over one thousand years ago," Momo said. "She is the very best list maker. The original. Number one."

Momo returned to her chair and rubbed the rag across the dish with increasing vigor. Getting a glimpse of the front, Yuki realized the dish was a mirror. The reflective side had a dark tarnished streak that looked like a storm cloud.

"That mirror looks antique," Yuki said. "Is that a *makkyu*, too?"

"*Makkyo*," Momo said, correcting her. "No, this is different."

Yuki leaned over the counter, trying to get a closer look. "How is it different?"

"It is not for sale," Momo said with a short, sharp laugh.

"No, really, how is it different?" Yuki asked.

Momo propped the mirror in a metal stand on the counter. Then she examined her reflection. "The writer I told you about? Sei Shōnagon? My great-grandparents owned a pawnshop. Not long after they opened the store, a man came in and said this mirror belonged to Shōnagon. He said once every hundred years or so, the mirror opens and takes you to her in the imperial palace. He said his daughter used to read the poems she wrote to the mirror. Then one day the daughter said she saw Shōnagon in the reflection and she disappeared into the mirror. This man could not stand to be reminded of his daughter's absence any longer. Of course, he could not prove any of this. Because we believe that spirits can become trapped inside a mirror, my great-grandparents kept it in a box. Eventually my parents closed the pawnshop. I came across the box and decided to keep the mirror. I liked the story. After my husband died, I thought if Shōnagon appeared, I would go visit her and have a new adventure. Now I check it every day."

"Why would anyone want to go back a thousand years?" Yuki said, puzzled. "We had to live like people in colonial times for a school project and it was awful. No lights, no TV, no microwave."

"Why?" Momo said indignantly. "Imagine you live in a palace and you do not have to go to school. All you do is write your lists, capturing the beauty around you. This is what Sei Shōnagon did. The imperial court dedicated their lives to beauty. Not like today, where all you do is look at your phone."

Yuki didn't think she'd want to travel to Sei Shōnagon's time. But she'd give anything for a mirror that would take her back four years, to the Saturday mornings when she and her father would get up while her mother slept in. They would made bread dough and pick a bouquet of flowers in the backyard. Then they'd crash on the sofa to work on a crossword puzzle, wrapped in the smell of warm bread and lilacs.

3

Even More Hateful Things

After she got home, Yuki put *The Pillow Book* on hold at the library. Then she logged into LVLup. Julio still hadn't responded to her question about Suzie, even though she could see he was on the site. Was he ignoring her or was he in the middle of a game? She tried to get his attention with another DM.

> CL4ever: Hey, Indiana Garcia-Jones! It's Snowbi-wan Kenobi. Nine days until our birthday! I found you a cool gift. I just have to get an advance on my allowance.

When he didn't reply, she kept going.

> CL4ever: Today's list is Top 5 Best Birthdays.

> CL4ever: No. 5 is the year I turned 10. That was the year my dad died and I didn't want to have a party but Hana made me. We went to Farrell's for ice cream and I ordered the Trough. I still have my ribbon that says "I made a pig of myself."

CL4ever: No. 4 is the year I turned 11. I had a haiku party. The other kids said it was like going to school. You're the only one who didn't complain.

As Yuki hit return, a message popped up on her screen.

Tig1010: Hola, Yukita! I'm not supposed to be here so keep it on the DL! I got busted for not doing homework. Don't get me anything too fancy, k? Cuz I already bought your gift. Mama's coming. Gotta jump!

Yuki typed faster, wanting to remind Julio that Suzie was a card thief and not to be trusted. But it was too late. He had logged off. Was the mirror too fancy? At least it would hang on the wall where he would see it every day, unlike a T-shirt that would get shoved into a drawer.

After going to the garage for a hammer and some nails, Yuki hung her mirror on the wall above her turntable. Then she swiveled in her desk chair and turned the flashlight on, off, on, off, making the lion appear and disappear.

Just past midnight, as she was drifting off to sleep, Yuki came up with a brilliant way to remind Julio of Suzie's past misdeeds. Logging in to LVLup again, she wrote a new list.

CL4ever: Hey, Hula Hoop! It's Yu-bik's Cube. Yesterday my science teacher Mr. Krash got annoyed with these kids in class and said, "You two better nip it in the butt." When I told him the saying was "nip it in the bud," he said, "What body part is the bud?" In honor of Mr. Krash (he's Russian, so English isn't his first language), here's my Top 5 People Who Should Be Nipped in the Butt:

1. This kid Zoe, who thinks she's cool and Goth but needs

29

to go back to kindergarten and learn how to tie her shoes and how to treat other people.

2. Ms. Ghosh, because diagramming sentences should be considered a crime against the English language.

3. My mom, for moving us to Santa Dolores.

4. Doug, who would be less annoying if he didn't try so hard.

5. Suzie, for being a Pokémon card thief.

Only eight days until our birthday!

A notification popped up on the screen, a DM from someone named BitterCress. *Hey! Isn't it past your bedtime?* Yuki zoomed in on BitterCress's photo. Was that Zoe? Alarmed that she had somehow summoned Zoe by bad-mouthing her, Yuki logged out and dove beneath the bedcovers.

In the morning, she checked LVLup again. Still no response from Julio. Thankfully Zoe had not sent her any more messages. When Yuki went downstairs, Hana was filling a thermos with hot tea.

"Yuki, I got an email from the library," her mother said. "Your book is ready. Why on earth did you check out *The Pillow Book* by Sei Shōnagon? In school, we had to practice writing Japanese characters by copying *The Pillow Book*. It was such a chore."

"I write lists and Shōnagon was the original list maker," Yuki said.

Hana nodded. "Ah. Yes, that makes sense."

Her mother should have made the connection when Yuki

first started writing her column for the school newspaper. But Hana didn't live and breathe books the way Yuki's father had. Her mother was something called a project manager, which seemed to involve a lot of spreadsheets and emails. Hana was the one who booked the dentist appointments, printed out and signed the forms for field trips, and separated the whites from the darks when doing laundry. Her father was the one who forgot to take Yuki to the dentist, sloshed coffee all over the permission slip, and threw a red sweatshirt in with the whites, thereby turning all the socks pink. Once, he had been so distracted thinking about the concept of home and why Dorothy would, as the scarecrow said, "wish to leave this beautiful country and go back to this dry, gray place you call Kansas," that he burned a pot of rice to a black crisp on the stove. The next day, Hana bought a rice cooker.

Pointing out that her father would have recommended *The Pillow Book* wasn't going to get Yuki an advance on her allowance, though. "Can I have another twenty-five dollars for Julio's gift? I'll wash your car this weekend," Yuki said.

Her mother balked. "What are you buying him that costs so much?"

"I want to get him a magic mirror like mine, only with a tiger," Yuki said.

Hana pursed her lips and Yuki could tell she was trying to be diplomatic, which was infuriating. "I'm glad you like your mirror," her mother said. "But are you sure he'll like it? He might prefer a video game. Or some nice art supplies."

"Everybody's going to get him video games and art supplies," Yuki said, crossing her arms. She knew it didn't sound like a great gift for an eighth grader. But she had to do something different from his other friends. Julio would love it once he saw the tiger.

"Good morning," Doug said, sidling between them to get to the coffee maker. "I've got a new one for you, Yuki. A doughnut walks into a bar. The bartender asks, 'How are things at the bakery?' And the doughnut says, 'Not good. I'm tired of the hole business.'"

Yuki rolled her eyes and poured Rice Krispies into a bowl.

"The *whole* business," Doug said. "Doughnuts have *holes*. Get it?"

"I get it, and I am *wholly* unimpressed," Yuki said.

Doug grinned and tapped his temple with his index finger. "I see what you did there."

Yuki turned back to her mother. "So can I have the twenty-five dollars?" she asked.

"Let's talk about it when I get home from work," Hana said with a grimace. "I just don't think it's the right gift for Julio."

Doug looked at Yuki and then at her mother. "What's going on?"

"She wants to get Julio one of those magic mirrors," Hana said, glancing at the clock. "I have to go. We'll talk about this later."

32

Her mother's heels clicked across the tile while Yuki looked down at the counter. Tears of frustration burned in her eyes.

"Have a good day, Yuki," Doug said, slapping his hand down as he turned to go.

When Yuki looked up, she found two twenties on the counter.

After the final bell brought another dreary week of school to a close, Yuki rode downtown to the library and picked up *The Pillow Book*. When she went to unlock her bike, she spotted Momo sweeping the sidewalk outside the emporium. Momo looked ready for a New Year's Eve party in a black sequined top and crystal teardrop earrings.

Yuki glided up to her on her bike. "Hi, Momo," she said. "Look what I got." Still straddling her bike, she pulled *The Pillow Book* out of her backpack. Momo leaned the broom against the wall.

"Let me see," Momo said. As she leafed through the pages, her eyes lit up. "It is like rereading a letter from an old friend. You must come back and tell me what you think of it."

"Yeah, sure," Yuki said. People often called her an old soul, and maybe that was her problem. She'd been born in the wrong decade. Her only friend in Santa Dolores was going to be an overdressed shopkeeper.

"I can buy the tiger mirror today," Yuki said.

"Okay, good," Momo said. "Let's go inside, then."

By the time Yuki finished locking her bike to a lamppost, Momo was encasing the mirror in bubble wrap. Yuki set her cash on the counter. While Momo counted out the change, Yuki remembered her English assignment. Maybe Momo would help her.

"For my English class, I'm supposed to interview someone," Yuki said. She had almost said, "someone old," but managed to stop herself. "It can be about a keepsake from your family. I wondered if I could write about you and Sei Shōnagon's mirror?"

"Yes, that is okay," Momo said with a shrug. "Shall we see if Shōnagon is here today?"

Yuki went behind the counter. Momo took the mirror out of a drawer and showed Yuki the back side, decorated with a droopy willow tree and a crane. Then she flipped it to the reflective side. "Hello, is anybody in there?" Momo said to the mirror.

Yuki peered over Momo's shoulder. But all she saw was Momo's dour face and a row of waving cats up on a shelf, either beckoning or warning them away.

Yuki read *The Pillow Book* late into the night and all Saturday morning. She loved Shōnagon's lists about depressing things, hateful things, things without merit, outstandingly splendid things, and things that made the heart grow fonder. She also loved the entries about life at court—what Yuki's teachers used to call "small moments"—about the cat who lived in the palace, about the palace guards twanging their bows during roll call, and why priests should be good-looking. The pillow in the title, Yuki learned, came from the wood pillows that the ladies used for sleeping. These pillows, headrests really, had drawers where a lady could store a ream of paper. That's where Shōnagon kept her writing—inside her wood pillow.

When she reached the last page, Yuki was filled with melancholy. She didn't want to be finished. No wonder Momo wanted to visit Shōnagon. The ladies and gentlemen of the court constantly wrote letters to one another like an ancient version of texting. Each exchange contained a poem, and each response built on the previous poem. Courtiers judged one another based on their letters. Yuki thought she'd be incredibly popular if those were the standards today.

Yuki was leaning against her reading pillow in bed, staring into space and savoring the spell of the book, when her mother came to the bedroom door.

"Doug's boss is having a barbecue this afternoon at the Ondulando Club," Hana said. "There will be kids from your school. You should come."

Yuki held the book up like a shield. "You guys go," she said. "I'd rather stay here."

Hana took a deep breath and said, "Yuki, I really think you should—"

"I said no," Yuki snapped. "Now please leave."

"Fine," Hana said, shutting the door.

The spell broken, Yuki went to her desk and checked LVLup. *The Pillow Book* had been a welcome distraction, keeping her from obsessively checking the chat. But now the temptation returned. When she saw a reply, she felt a rush of excitement.

Tig1010: I think you'd like Suzie now if you gave her a chance. Once I ate a box of Girl Scout cookies that my sister was selling and I lied about it and then my mom found the plastic cookie sleeve in my room. So see, I've done stupid stuff, too.

Yes, but you're a good person and Suzie is not, Yuki typed. As her index finger hovered over the return key, she heard her father ask, *Are you pulling someone closer or pushing them away?* With a sigh, she deleted her comment and typed a new message.

CL4ever: Sounds like Suzie's taken my place.

Yuki felt hollow inside. After the Pokémon card incident, she had complained to her father that even though she'd done the right thing, everyone except for Julio had turned on her for telling the teacher. "You only need one friend," her father had said, patting her on the back. Now she didn't even have one.

Opening a blank document on the computer, Yuki threw herself into the only thing that made her feel good—writing. *Every day, Momo Fujita polishes a mirror once owned by the famous Japanese writer Sei Shōnagon. Momo got the mirror from her great-grandparents' pawnshop.* Yuki frowned. Boring. She kept writing and deleting. Now she didn't even enjoy writing. Santa Dolores had ruined everything. She opened *The Pillow Book* to random pages, trying to find inspiration.

She liked Shōnagon's gossipy enthusiasm, like she was confiding to a friend. Yuki could also relate to the feelings that Shōnagon expressed: *What a delight it is when Her Majesty summons me to her side so that all the others have to make way!* And: *One is in a hurry to leave, but one's visitor keeps chattering away . . . the situation is hateful indeed.* And: *Letters are commonplace enough, yet what splendid things they are!* If only Julio felt the same.

Yuki thought about how Shōnagon might describe her mirror. *The mirror on my vanity is decorated with a crane and a drooping willow tree. It has a cloudy spot on the reflective side that I find most charming. I have spent many hours in front of my mirror, for a lady-in-waiting serving the empress must always look her best. Perhaps that is why, after I passed away, my spirit lived on inside the mirror. But every hundred years, I get bored and invite someone to come join me. Most delightful!*

Yuki wrote her whole paper in Shōnagon's voice. She couldn't wait to turn it in.

School that week was more of the same. In social studies, Yuki continued to write her group's Egyptian gods skit by herself. In science, Mr. Krash threatened to make them dissect worms if they didn't behave, while in English, Ms. Ghosh made them diagram more sentences. Then on Thursday, Ms. Ghosh called up five students to read their stories out loud to the class. But she didn't include Yuki. The disappointment stung. Teachers always held her up as an example. What had gone wrong? Afterward, Ms. Ghosh called up the rest of the students to her desk one by one to discuss their papers. She asked for Yuki last.

Ms. Ghosh looked at her over the top of her glasses. "Your story was very confusing," she said. "This doesn't seem to be told from Mumu's perspective."

"Momo," Yuki said, even though she knew she probably shouldn't correct her teacher. "I was trying to sound like Sei Shōnagon, the one who the mirror originally belonged to."

Ms. Ghosh sniffed. "Why would you do that?"

Yuki was so accustomed to praise from teachers that the question stunned her. "I don't know. I was trying to be creative," she said in a small voice.

Ms. Ghosh handed her the marked-up paper with a 48 at the top. An F. Yuki had never received anything less than an A ever. "This is supposed to be about what the mirror means to Mumu, not to Polygon," she said. "I'll give you until Monday to turn in a new one."

If Shōnagon were here, she'd categorize this moment under "incredibly distressing things" and Ms. Ghosh as "most unpleasant." So angry she was ready to cry, Yuki plowed through the crowded hallway. A hand fell on her arm. "Hey, are you okay?" Zoe asked. Yuki shook her off and pushed open the door. Racing home on her bike, she almost ran over a little kid in the crosswalk and swerved around a car backing out of a driveway. At the house, she ran upstairs to her mother's bedroom to use the paper shredder next to the desk. Yuki couldn't wait to turn the giant red 48 into confetti. But halfway through, the machine gagged.

Crouching by the desk, Yuki reversed the feed and pulled out her half-eaten paper. Then something white in the trash bin next to the shredder caught her eye. She'd seen enough pregnancy tests in ads to know what one looked like. Yuki picked up the white wand and stared at the pink plus sign in the window. Hana couldn't have another baby, could she? Her mother was old! She was forty-one! Yuki's chest heaved, and there was a high-pitched ringing in her ears. If her mother and Doug had their own kid, Yuki was going to be invisible even in her own family.

Yuki dropped the test back in the trash. Clutching what remained of her paper, she ran to her bedroom and started to sob. She wanted her father. She would never stop missing him. One day she had left for school as usual and by the time she'd gotten home, he was gone forever. His last words to her hadn't been deep or loving. In fact, he had lectured her for putting the milk back in the refrigerator with only a splash left in the bottom. "It wasn't completely empty," she had said in her defense. "Oh, stuff and nonsense," he'd retorted. She was still upset that they'd had a stupid argument over the milk and then he died. It wasn't fair.

The only other person who understood her was Julio. She would beg Julio to call her if she had to. But when she opened LVLup, Yuki thought she'd clicked on the wrong chat.

Tig1010: Hey pal, no way did I replace you! I got the Buena Vista gang here. They want to say hi.

Legend_of_Troy: What up, Yuki? The BV isn't the same since you left.

SiouxieRocks: Hey, Yuki. Wow, you're still writing your lists! I can't believe you remember all this stuff from elementary school. Next time you're on, let's play Wordler!

Tig1010: We gotta plot Doug's downfall so you can move back—ha ha!

Yuki rubbed her eyes. Then she refreshed the page. This all had to be a bad dream. But no, Julio had invited Troy and Suzie, and the only list that Yuki had written lately was the one about who should get nipped in the butt. Her mouth went dry.

CL4ever: Julio, I'm calling you right now and you better pick up.

She ran downstairs and dialed Julio from the phone in the kitchen.

"Hola, Yukita," he said. "What's going on?"

"What's going on?" she said, outraged. "You added Troy and Suzie to our chat."

Julio cleared his throat. "I thought it might make you feel better to see that we're all thinking about you. I was trying to cheer you up."

"But that was private," she said, horrified. "Did you tell Suzie that I said she should be nipped in the butt?" Hana always said the problem with social media was that people wrote things they would never dare say face-to-face. She hated that her mother was right.

40

"I showed Suzie your list and she thought it was funny," he said. "She's not mad."

Julio kept talking but Yuki didn't hear the rest. It was like watching blood gush from a paper cut and remembering how sharp and painful a piece of paper could be. After they hung up, Yuki grabbed the tiger mirror from her bedroom. There would be no dinner. There would be no special birthday gift. She was going to get her money back.

On the way to Momo's store, Yuki compiled a list of hateful things: *Stepping in dog poop with brand-new sneakers. Julio. Teachers who give you a 48 even though you worked really hard. Julio. Moms who remarry, make you move, and have another baby. Julio. Julio. Julio.*

Yuki marched into the Rising Sun Emporium and set the mirror on the counter. "My friend is no longer my friend," she said. "I need to return this."

Momo pointed to a handwritten sign next to the register. "All sales final," she said.

Yuki's face fell. "But I spent my whole allowance," she said.

"That is the rule," Momo said.

Momo hadn't even asked what happened. That was the last blow. In that moment, Yuki was Alice flailing at the pack of cards and Dorothy discovering that the Wizard of Oz was a terrible humbug. "I hate this place," Yuki shrieked. "I hate Santa Dolores and everyone in it." Then she burst into tears.

Momo, flummoxed, took Yuki by the arm and led her to a

stool behind the counter. "Okay, okay. Come sit and we will talk. I will make you some tea."

Sobs convulsed Yuki, forcing loud, ugly sounds out of her mouth. She couldn't remember ever crying like this, even when her father died. She'd been too shocked and scared to cry then.

As Momo set the kettle on the hot plate, the bell above the door jingled. "Hello! Could I get a closer look at this?" a man asked. Momo rushed over to help him while Yuki wiped her tears and gazed at her splotchy face in the mirror. She rubbed her chin, trying to remove a dirty spot. Then she realized the spot was not on her face but on the mirror. The dark cloud kept growing, billowing across her reflection until it filled the entire surface. Then the roiling mass dissolved and Yuki froze. The face staring back at her was not her own. The woman looked like the old-fashioned Japanese doll Yuki's mother kept in a glass case in the living room. Her layered robes, light greens with hints of orange and white, formed a striped V on her chest. Sleek black hair framed a face painted stark white. And where her eyebrows should have been, the woman had two charcoal smudges. Could this be Sei Shōnagon?

"Momo," Yuki called out.

The mirror quivered, expanding from the size of a dinner plate to that of a large pizza. Yuki touched the surface, which felt pliant like Jell-O. Suddenly she felt an irresistible tug, like a rip current in the ocean on a hot summer day.

Then the stranger in the mirror tilted her head, gave her an alluring smile, and held out her hand. Her long, elegant fingers peeked out from her bell-shaped sleeve, and she waved at Yuki as if to say "come."

4

On the Other Side of the Mirror

The mirror trembled and stretched until it formed an oval door. Sei Shōnagon—for that's who Yuki decided the mysterious lady had to be—nodded and reached for her. Yuki had longed for an escape from Santa Dolores, and now the mirror was offering her one. The mirror encased Yuki's hands up to her wrists and the inside felt cool and inviting like silk. Shōnagon continued to beckon, her sleeves spreading like butterfly wings.

"Yuki, what are you doing?" Momo said. "Put the mirror down."

"I can't," Yuki said, mesmerized by the warmth and intelligence that Shōnagon exuded. "She's so beautiful."

"What do you mean?" Momo came up behind her. "What do you see?"

The mirror shimmered and pulled her inside up to her elbows. If she went, Yuki would be taking away the opportunity from Momo. But Momo couldn't see Shōnagon. And what if the mirror didn't open again for another century?

"I see Shōnagon," Yuki said. "She wants me to come to the other side."

"This is not funny," Momo said. "Put the mirror down."

But already Momo sounded far away. Yuki took a step forward and held her breath as she passed into the mirror. A softness enveloped her, and the air turned a coppery-tinged blue. From the outside, it had looked like Yuki could step straight into Shōnagon's room. That's how it had worked in *Through the Looking-Glass*. Alice had passed through the mirror as if she'd climbed through a window. But from the inside, Shōnagon appeared to stand at the end of a tunnel. Yuki took another step and felt a heavy resistance all around her, like she was in a swimming pool. Each slow-motion stride set off ripples that one moment gave Shōnagon a huge balloon head and skinny body like a Japanese *kokeshi* doll and the next moment bloated her lower body, turning her into a batik bowling pin. After a few steps, Yuki could no longer hold her breath. But when her lips broke apart, she did not swallow water. Instead, the air was deliciously cool and soothing. Yuki figured out that if she pushed off the ball of her foot and floated forward with each step, it was less tiring.

Coming to a fork in the tunnel, Yuki saw Shōnagon to her left and her mother, a younger version of her mother, to the right. There was something so carefree about Hana in a flowy turquoise dress with her hair in a high ponytail that Yuki took an involuntary step toward her. Suddenly she was face-to-face with Hana, who had crouched in front of her on the sidewalk. They were outside a supermarket, and her mother was holding up a Kit Kat bar. "Yuki, you can't take candy without paying for it. That's called stealing. We're going back inside and you are going to apologize." Yuki felt the burn of shame work its way from her chest up to her ears. Then something large and eely rippled behind her mother. Yuki jerked backward and saw the scene before her as if in a movie, her mother kneeling in front of her three-year-old self. Then another ripple cut across the supermarket windows. The front of the creature looked like a breaking wave, with sea-foam forming a dragon-like head and claws. Yuki turned around and ran. Whatever that dragony thing was, she didn't want to get too close to it.

When she reached the fork, she stopped. Where was Shōnagon? She thought she saw a blurry form and headed toward it. The blurry form became Julio, waving from the ladder of the swing set in his backyard. He was in his soccer uniform, and when he smiled, his two front teeth were missing. Yuki felt her body whoosh forward. Glancing down at her clothes, she saw she was wearing her blue Catbus T-shirt, which meant she had to be in second grade. Julio scrambled up the ladder to the top of the swing set. "I'm going to be Ant-Man for Halloween," he announced as he stood up and balanced on the rails. Yuki felt tears well in her eyes. "But we always do *The Wizard of* Oz," she said, looking up at him from the lawn because she was afraid to climb to the top. "I'm going to be Ant-Man and you can be the Wasp," Julio said. Before she could reply, the water dragon whipped around him and came straight at her. Yuki pulled out of her younger self and ran.

This time when Yuki came to the fork, she saw Shōnagon again, holding out her hand and looking at her with an encouraging smile. Yuki kept her eyes fixed on Shōnagon as she half swam, half ran toward her. She didn't like the other places the mirror was taking her to, anyway. Behind her, Yuki heard something swish and hoped the water dragon didn't bite. Suddenly she heard her father's voice call out. As she whipped her head to the left, another passageway appeared. Her heart jumped when she saw her father as he had looked on his last day, dressed in a swirly purple sweatshirt with the Cheshire Cat saying "We're all mad here" and balancing on a pair of crutches in front of the open refrigerator. She rushed toward him. Maybe she could apologize and change the last thing she said to him. As she snapped into her nine-year-old self, her father held up the milk carton. "There's no milk in here," he said crossly. "If you finish the milk, don't put it back in the refrigerator."

Say you're sorry, Yuki told herself. *He's going to die and you're never going to see him again.* But her nine-year-old self didn't listen. "It's not completely empty," she said. "There's still enough for Mom's coffee."

Yuki felt a crushing despair. Why had she been so

determined to be right when her dad was probably in pain from his knee surgery? Why hadn't she been nicer? This time the ripples appeared in two places, above the kitchen cabinets and along the countertop. Two water dragons came at her with their sea-foam teeth bared. Yuki pulled out of her nine-year-old self and ran back to the split in the tunnel, praying that Shōnagon was still there. She didn't want to be inside the mirror anymore. And she definitely didn't want to go home.

Glancing over her shoulder, she saw the two sea-foam dragons forming a wave that threatened to break over her head. She forced herself to move faster, pushing off harder and floating farther with each step. At the fork, she was relieved to find Shōnagon down the tunnel to the right and waiting with a serene air. Rushing toward her, Yuki burst through the other side of the mirror and landed on hands and knees on a polished wood floor.

Yuki got to her feet and stood before Shōnagon in a small, simple room that had three paneled walls. The fourth was covered by a floor-to-ceiling woven blind. Yuki turned around to make sure the dragony things hadn't followed her through the mirror. But she could not see the strange creatures or Momo's store. The mirror rested on a low vanity in a metal stand and reflected back the brushes and ceramic pots scattered across the surface. With a shiver, Yuki realized the portal had closed.

"Look at you," Shōnagon exclaimed.

Yuki whirled around and gaped. Shōnagon was short, coming up only to Yuki's chin, and had eyes the color of maple syrup. Shōnagon appeared younger than Yuki's mother, but old enough to be a mother. Her light green outer robe was patterned with flowers in white, purple, and orange, and she wore this over plain silk robes in different shades of green, burnt orange, and white, layered so that the edges showed at the neckline and at the hem of her sleeves. Though she was dainty, there was something commanding about her.

"I am at a loss for words, and I am never at a loss for words," Shōnagon said.

Yuki realized Shōnagon had spoken in Japanese, or at least what sounded like Japanese to her ear. Yet somehow Yuki had understood every word.

"Are you . . ." Yuki paused, amazed that the words coming out of her own mouth also seemed to be Japanese. She couldn't have gone back in time, then, to the turn of the eleventh century. She must have crossed into another dimension, as Alice had. Otherwise, how could she speak Japanese?

"Are you Sei Shōnagon, author of *The Pillow Book*?" Yuki asked.

Shōnagon clapped her hands. "I am still known," she said. "Isn't that splendid? Now, what is your name, dear?"

"Yuki Snow," she said. But she knew Shōnagon heard *Yuki Yuki*. How she wished her parents had given her a different name! Of course, back home nobody had known that her first name meant "snow" in Japanese. But when she went to

Japan, most of them knew enough English to realize. Even though the laughter had been lighthearted, she found her double name embarrassing all the same.

"Yuki Yuki," Shōnagon said. "That is a delightful name. Nothing is more beautiful than moonlight shining on a snow-covered roof. Even the hut of a peasant is improved. Oh, I must write that down."

She rushed over and knelt in front of what Yuki determined must be a legless desk near the woven blind. Opening a square box, Shōnagon picked up a brush, dipped it into a divot filled with ink, and wrote swiftly. "Things that are improved by a dusting of snow," she said. "A mountain reflected in a lake. A grove of pine trees. The hunting cloak of a gentleman who has braved a storm to visit a lady. The huts of commoners in the moonlight. See, Yuki, already you've inspired me."

Yuki wasn't sure that making fun of commoners was the type of thing she wanted to inspire. Especially since she would be a commoner in Shōnagon's eyes. It wasn't like she came from a mansion in Beverly Hills.

"I write lists, too," Yuki said shyly. Not that hers would make any sense to Shōnagon. Like "Top Five Reasons Why Sailor Moon Is *Shika Katan* (the Best)" and "Top 5 J-Pop Songs to Play on Repeat."

Shōnagon went to a small wood chest the size of a jewelry box that had been left on the floor. Opening a drawer, Shōnagon dropped the page inside. Yuki noticed the box was oddly shaped, like a trapezoid. Then she realized it wasn't a jewelry box at all. It was an ancient Japanese pillow! She was looking at the headrest that gave *The Pillow Book* its name. If her mother were here, she'd make Hana take a photo with her phone. That had been on Yuki's list of reasons why she should have a phone: so that she could take her own photos. Then she'd have proof that she'd been with Shōnagon at the imperial court when she went home.

"Well, the wave snakes must be doing their jobs," Shōnagon said. "You emerged very quickly."

"So that's what those things were," Yuki said. "I thought they were dragons. I saw some old memories in there, too, of my parents and my best friend."

"Of course you did," Shōnagon said. "You were inside a mirror. Those were your reflections. But sometimes our visitors get lost in their memories and it's up to the wave snakes to bring them here."

"They weren't good memories, so I didn't mind leaving," Yuki said.

"Now tell me about the fashions in your time," Shōnagon said, pinching the fabric of Yuki's blue-and-white-striped T-shirt between her fingers. "I've never seen an outfit like this before. And your hair! It's short, like a nun's."

Yuki looked down at her hair, which now reached her chest after she'd refused to cut it all summer. She supposed that was short by Shōnagon's standards. But Shōnagon didn't give her time to answer.

"Are you from the new capital of Tokyo?" Shōnagon continued. "That is where my last visitor came from. It is nothing more than a fishing village right now, you know."

"My mother was born in Tokyo, but she moved across the ocean to a country called America," Yuki said. "That's where I'm from. Your mirror is now there, too."

"My mirror went across the sea," Shōnagon said. "Astonishing. And how did it come into your possession in the Land of a Merry Cat?"

Yuki thought of the waving cats in Momo's store and bit her lip to keep herself from laughing. Thankfully Shōnagon was distracted by a knock on the door, which gave Yuki a chance to swallow the giggle that threatened to come out. Shōnagon slid open a panel to reveal a girl around Yuki's age with a pert mouth and serious eyes that radiated confidence. The girl was dressed like Shōnagon, in layered floor-length robes, only hers were in bright yellows and dark greens.

"Come in, quickly," Shōnagon said, ushering the girl inside and closing the door. "Izumi, this is Yuki."

"It's nice to meet you. I love your name," Yuki said. If only her mother had named her Izumi, then she could have gone by Izzy. Hana really should have thought this through.

Izumi stepped around Shōnagon and recoiled. "Shōnagon, she's not—I mean."

Yuki braced for her to say "not Japanese." When she visited Japan with her mother, Yuki had quickly learned that her relatives did not think of her as half Japanese. They thought of her as one hundred percent American. Hana's relatives also kept asking if her mother could still read kanji, the Japanese writing system adapted from Chinese characters, and Yuki had the feeling they didn't think of her mother as fully Japanese anymore, either.

"Nobody has ever come through not wearing a robe," Izumi said.

Yuki looked down at her T-shirt, jeans, and white sneakers. She might as well have been in a green alien costume.

"Yes, it appears much has changed since our last visitor," Shōnagon said. "Yuki is from the Land of a Merry Cat."

Izumi gasped. "She's a foreigner? How can she be a contestant?"

"Now, Izumi, we know nothing about her yet," Shōnagon said. "You must be patient. Remember, our last contestant had gone to school, and we were shocked by that."

"She did, and she still had much to learn for the contest," Izumi said. "How can we possibly prepare a foreigner?"

"It's a reminder of how fortunate we are here at court to be steeped in poetry at all times," Shōnagon said. "All our contestants have needed to prepare, no matter what time or place they came from."

"Of course," Izumi said, wringing her hands. "It's only that we're already behind."

"What kind of contest?" Yuki asked. She had crossed through the mirror on impulse, thinking she would get a vacation from her life. It should have occurred to her that neither Alice nor Dorothy got to chill out. Alice immediately set off across the chessboard and Dorothy had to go find the Wizard of Oz. Yuki hoped she didn't have to walk a long distance for the contest. She had never liked hiking.

"You've been brought to us through the mirror for the express purpose of becoming our next high priestess of poetry," Shōnagon said. "It's a great honor."

High priestess of poetry? That sounded important. "I'm almost thirteen," Yuki said. "Am I old enough to be a high priestess?"

"You are the exact right age," Shōnagon said, batting away the question with a wave of her hand.

"How many contestants are there?" Yuki asked. She had always wanted to do another Wonderland Slam. But after her father died, it had been too painful to return to campus.

"Only two," Shōnagon said. "You will represent Empress Teishi. The other contestant will compete on behalf of the imperial consort, Shōshi."

"What is a consort?" Yuki asked.

"The consort is the emperor's second wife," Shōnagon said. "The emperor can have as many wives as he would like. But there can be only one empress. However, the title of empress alone is not enough. A woman must wield influence at court, and that is why this contest matters. The winner is held in high esteem. Therefore, finding the best contestant is of the utmost importance. My mirror invites the young lady with the most artistic spirit to cross over."

"Does the consort's contestant also come through a mirror?" Yuki asked, worried that Izumi might be right. Even if the other contestant came from the twenty-first century, Yuki being a foreigner might be a huge disadvantage.

Shōnagon turned away and rummaged inside a large wooden chest. "I suspect she does," she said, though her words seemed to have a nervous edge. "Once we leave this room, you must not tell anyone about the mirror or that you have come from another century. The rest of the court believes the contestants are girls from the provinces. Of course, both sides do what they can to gain an advantage. Among Empress Teishi's ladies, Izumi and I are the only ones who know the truth. If anyone asks, you traveled from the Land of a Merry Cat by ship. They will attribute your eccentricities to the fact that you are a foreigner."

Yuki nodded. Between the contest and the secrecy around the mirror, her head was spinning. As Shōnagon took some clothes out of the chest, the blind rippled and a golden bird about the size of a chicken burst into the room. Then a much larger animal crashed through the blind, a floppy brown-and-white dog with oversize paws. The dog chased the bird in dizzying circles, knocking over a robe stand in the corner. Yuki let out a startled yelp. Shōnagon and Izumi shrieked.

"My lady, permission to enter please," a boy called out from behind the blind.

"Yes, Nobu, yes," Shōnagon cried. "Please do something about this tempest."

A lanky boy of about twelve or thirteen slipped inside, his black cap askew and dusty paw prints all over his tunic and loose trousers. Even amid the commotion, Yuki noted Nobu's bright hazel eyes, his high cheekbones, and the graceful way he moved around the room. In the Valley, he'd be one of those kids who was always leaving school early to go to auditions.

"Okinamaro, stop this at once," he said as he tried to grab the silk rope tied around the dog's neck. But the dog danced out of reach.

Shōnagon pulled Yuki and Izumi close to her and they huddled together as bird, dog, and boy whirled around them. With a squawk, the bird darted outside again. The dog and the boy bounded after it. Then Shōnagon rushed over to the blind and pulled it back, revealing a wood veranda shaded by deep eaves. A short flight of stairs led down to a court-yard garden, where the bird half flew and half ran while the dog barked up a joyous storm and Nobu shouted "Okina-maro, come back!" Then six fierce-looking men in dark gray tunics—guards, if Yuki had to guess—entered the courtyard and joined the chase, one trying to catch the bird with a large net and the rest trying to grab the dog. Okinamaro seemed to think this was great fun, drawing them in and then leap-ing away at the last second. Finally, a guard managed to lasso the dog with a rope. Another guard clamped his hand on Nobu's shoulder. The bird remained free, perching on the sloping roof of the building across the courtyard.

Shōnagon dropped the blind. "Poor Nobu," she said. "The emperor's dog is such a nuisance."

"What does Nobu do, besides chase the dog?" Yuki asked.

Izumi rolled her eyes. "Unbelievable," she said. "You've only just arrived and already you're swooning over a page boy."

Yuki felt her face grow hot. Nobu was good-looking. That was a fact. At home, she had been like Izumi, rolling her eyes when she overheard girls in class gossiping about who was cute and who was not. She hadn't been the cool kid like Suzie who got caught passing flirty notes during a typing exercise. But nobody here knew that about her. Maybe she could be that kid here.

"I am not swooning," Yuki said. "I'm asking what he does at court."

"Don't mind Izumi," Shōnagon said, returning the robe stand to an upright position. "One day she will look up from her books and appreciate being in the presence of a hand-some young person like Nobu."

"Even a preacher ought to be good-looking," Yuki said, quoting Shōnagon to Shōnagon.

"Did I write that?" Shōnagon said with a droll smile. "How clever of me."

Pulling back the edge of the blind and peering outside, Yuki watched a guard climb a bamboo ladder up to the roof where the bird was perched. It was a beautiful bird, with a golden head, a bright red chest, and blue markings on its wings.

57

"The empress will be very upset that her golden pheasant has escaped," Izumi said, peeking around the other side of the blind. "That's her favorite bird."

The guard crawled up the roof toward the pheasant. When he had almost reached the peak, the bird fluttered to the ground. Yuki giggled as the guard cursed.

Shōnagon handed Yuki a long-sleeved white robe and a pleated red trouser skirt and told her to change behind a folding screen. Behind the screen, Yuki held up the white robe, which went down to her knees. Through a crack between the panels of the screen, she studied Izumi and Shōnagon. The white robe appeared to be the first layer of their outfits and was worn tucked inside the high-waisted pants. As she changed, she listened to Izumi and Shōnagon conferring.

"We should present her to the empress at once," Shōnagon said. "She'll be relieved by the news. The other contestant has been here already for several days."

"I came to fetch you," Izumi said. "The empress wants you to join her in the emperor's quarters."

"Well, we must hurry, then," Shōnagon said. "No time for makeup. We'll just dress Yuki and comb out her hair."

When Yuki emerged from behind the screen, Shōnagon draped several light pink, mint-green, and white robes on her, adjusting each layer so that a thin sliver of the fabric showed at the neckline and at the bottom of her sleeves. Finally, Shōnagon placed a floral-patterned green robe on top of all the layers. During their Japan trip, Hana had taken

Yuki to a studio where they dressed her in a kimono and then took her photo. Yuki wasn't sure which was less comfortable, the kimono's wide belt, which had been wrapped around her midsection like a tourniquet, or the weight of all these loose flowing robes that had been heaped on her. She sat on a stool in front of the vanity while Izumi combed her hair, parting it down the middle.

"She still looks like a foreigner," Izumi said with concern. "It will cause quite a stir."

"She'll hold up a fan in front of her face and we'll sit apart from the other ladies," Shōnagon said. "There's nothing else to be done."

Shōnagon handed her a fan with a tree and a bird painted on it. When they left the room, Shōnagon and Izumi seemed to glide down the hall, their floor-length hair pooling in the trains of their robes. The weight of their outfits didn't seem to affect them at all. Yuki struggled to keep up with them, leaning forward like a draft horse pulling a wagon.

Izumi explained the layout of the palace as they walked. The wing with Shōnagon's room housed all the empress's attendants. The building on the opposite side of the courtyard, where the pheasant had perched, was where the consort's attendants stayed. As they passed through a covered outdoor hallway that connected the attendants' wing to the empress's quarters, Yuki noticed the buildings were uniform, single-story structures on raised platforms, with verandas and deep eaves. The consort lived in the wing across from the empress's, Izumi told her, and the building between them at the far end housed the emperor. Once they entered the empress's quarters, Shōnagon led them along a veranda that overlooked a garden. Near the emperor's quarters rose a white mountain that appeared to be made of snow. The mountain was flanked by a blooming cherry tree on one side and a fiery red maple on the other.

"What season is it?" Yuki asked, amazed that all three could be present at the same time.

"We have the best of all seasons here at the palace," Izumi said proudly.

That seemed like another clue that Yuki had traveled to another dimension and not back in time. The thought made her uneasy. She couldn't count on knowing how things worked here. "How does the snow not melt when it's so warm out?" she asked.

"The gardeners bring fresh snow several times a day," Shōnagon said. "I find it most delightful to watch them work."

As they walked along the veranda, Yuki peeked inside the rooms whenever the breeze fluttered the lowered blinds. A group of women sewed large fabric panels in one room while a teacher led a group of young girls in a writing exercise in another. The little girls wore robes in bright pastels. Though she had read descriptions of the palace and how people at court dressed in *The Pillow Book*, Yuki still felt disoriented. Dorothy must have felt the same way when she emerged from her house in Munchkinland. In the book, Dorothy really went to Oz and back. But in the movie, Dorothy had dreamed the whole thing. Yuki wondered which was happening to her. Maybe she was asleep in her bed and the paper, the LVLup chat, and the pregnancy test had all been part of a bad dream.

As they crossed another covered walkway to the emperor's quarters, Yuki got a closer look at the snow mountain. At the base was a lotus pond bursting with water lily pads and sharp-tipped flowers. The cherry and maple trees on either side had dropped such a perfect scattering of petals and leaves that Yuki wondered if someone was assigned to sprinkle them on the ground.

Inside the emperor's quarters, they entered a reception room, where a row of male courtiers in bulky dark robes and tall black caps faced a low platform. All the ladies appeared to be behind portable curtains that had been set up along the sides of the room. Shōnagon led them to a curtain near a wood pillar and motioned for Yuki to sit between her and Izumi. Using her fan, Shōnagon widened the crack between the curtain panels so they could peer out.

"That is Consort Shōshi," Shōnagon said.

Yuki followed Shōnagon's gaze and caught a glimpse of a teenage girl approaching a set of curtains on the other side.

"Keep in mind that the empress and the consort are cousins, but theirs is not a friendly relationship," Shōnagon added.

Yuki nodded. She didn't remember a rivalry in *The Pillow*

Book, but maybe those references had gone over her head. Up on the platform, a boy in his late teens emerged from behind a gold screen and knelt on a silk cushion. He wore a crimson tunic and had a pudgy face, an upturned nose, and eyes that were set too close together. His preening air reminded her of Suzie.

"Is that Emperor Ichijō? He looks so young," Yuki said.

"The emperors are always young, for that is how Regent Fujiwara stays in power," Shōnagon explained. "Once the emperor has a male heir, the regent will make sure the emperor retires and then his son will be elevated to the throne. But don't ever repeat that. Also, remember that Regent Fujiwara is Empress Teishi's uncle and Consort Shōshi's father. The empress does not get along with him."

Yuki thought the empress's family drama sounded intense. Today they'd be a reality show called *Following Up with the Fujiwaras*. "Why don't they get along?" Yuki asked.

"The empress backed her brother for regent," Shōnagon said. "When her uncle took power, he exiled the empress's brother to the Tedium."

"The Tedium?" Yuki repeated. "What's that?"

Izumi shuddered. "The Tedium is a province shrouded in a thick fog," she said. "That's where people who have been banished from the capital are sent. They are forced to live among demons, ogres, and other monsters. It's a horrible place."

The Tedium sounded like something that would exist in an alternate dimension. Unless this province simply had weather patterns like San Francisco, which was always socked with fog.

"But the empress is safe? The regent can't banish her?" Yuki asked.

"No, he won't banish her," Shōnagon said. "Instead he is trying to undermine her by reducing her influence at court. He is doing everything in his power to make his daughter, the consort, the emperor's favorite, for that increases his own power."

"The regent sounds very unpleasant," Yuki said. At least Doug tried to get her to like him.

"Yes, I would list their family relations under 'things that are troubling,'" Shōnagon said. "However, the regent seems to relish pitting everyone against each other, so the situation is not troubling to *him*."

Izumi nudged Yuki with her elbow. "There's the empress," she said.

Based on how Shōnagon described the empress in *The Pillow Book*, Yuki had expected to see an impossibly magical being, like Glinda the Good Witch, floating around in a luminous bubble. Instead, she saw a teenage girl in scarlet robes joining the emperor on the dais. She had sleek shiny hair that pooled in the train of her robes. An ornament twisted into the shape of an abstract flower perched on top of her head. Something about how she carried herself made her seem more mature than the emperor.

The chatter that filled the room was suddenly drowned out by a barking dog. Okinamaro bounded toward the dais, straining against the rope tied around his neck and dragging a guard with him. Another guard brought Nobu into the room. When they neared the dais, Okinamaro lay down and barked, his tail thumping against the floor. Nobu stood with his shoulders back and his head bowed. A long lock of hair had escaped from his cap and cascaded over his forehead. Yuki found his humble and earnest expression appealing.

"Your Royal Majesties," said the guard next to Nobu. "We regret to report that this afternoon the royal dog, Okinamaro, got away from this page boy. Okinamaro then opened the cage of the golden pheasant and proceeded to chase the bird, causing mayhem throughout the palace. Not only did Okinamaro knock over a vat of violet clothing dye, but he tracked purple paw prints throughout the imperial dining room, and also trampled the royal herb garden."

"Have you found my pheasant?" the empress asked.

"Not yet, my lady," the guard said. "We have not given up."

"Your report is most vexing," Emperor Ichijō said. "Page boy, I feel I can no longer count on you to look after Okinamaro."

"I have failed in my duties, Your Majesty," Nobu said with his eyes cast down.

"Okinamaro, for your insubordination, you are banished to the Tedium," the emperor said.

Yuki took in a sharp breath. That seemed like a cruel thing to do to a dog. Okinamaro howled, as if he knew he'd been punished. Then the emperor addressed Nobu. "Page boy, since you have proven yourself unfit to care for the royal dog, you are to be decapitated at once."

Nobu blanched. A murmur ran through the hall. Yuki couldn't believe her ears. Death seemed too harsh a punishment. Something must have been lost in translation. She looked at Shōnagon with disbelief.

"Not to worry," Shōnagon whispered. "The emperor will surely change his mind."

"My dear husband," the empress said. "While I am devastated that I may never see my pheasant again, I believe Okinamaro is the party most responsible for this unfortunate turn of events."

"The page boys have been lax in their duties of late," the emperor said. "That is exactly why this one must be decapitated. We must send a message that laziness will not be tolerated."

"Perhaps this could wait until morning," the empress said. "One of my ladies has composed a poem for the regent to welcome him back from his pilgrimage, and the girls are ready to perform a dance. My uncle would no doubt like to enjoy the festivities and not be immediately thrust into such grim matters. He'll be here at any moment."

The emperor's face turned bright red. "I am the one who decides, not the regent," he sputtered. "Your poetry and your dances will have to wait."

Yuki felt sorry for the empress. She seemed to be trying very hard to get the emperor to do the right thing while also trying not to make him angry. The empress scanned the gentlemen in the audience for help. But none of them said a word.

Shōnagon sighed. "Izumi, please let the regent know that his presence is urgently requested," she said. Then she stood up and approached the dais as Izumi rushed off, leaving Yuki alone behind the curtain.

"Your Majesty, if I may speak, Okinamaro's behavior was inexcusable," Shōnagon said. "But he is a puppy, and a sweet dog who has brought much joy to the royal household. He will never survive on his own in the Tedium. At least send Nobu with him as his caretaker."

"My decision stands," the emperor said. "Guards, take the page boy to the decapitation chamber and call for the master of divination at once."

Two guards took Nobu by the arms. Could the regent get here in time to stop them? Maybe the imperial court was like Wonderland, where the Queen of Hearts shouted "Off with his head!" but the beheading never took place. But how could Yuki be sure? As the guards led Nobu away, Yuki stepped out from behind the curtain and cried, "Wait!"

5

The Stranger in the Prophecy

On the day of the Pokémon card incident, Yuki had returned from an errand to the school office to find Suzie in the cubby area, taking two Pokémon cards from Maddie's backpack and slipping them into her sweatshirt pocket. After Yuki told the teacher what she saw, Ms. Marybeth had sighed and made Suzie return the cards to Maddie. Later, in the lunch line, Suzie had hissed, "Tattletale." Maddie'd had the nerve to laugh and say, "Yeah, Yuki's a tattletale." Then a group of boys had kept shouting, "Narc!" All Yuki wanted was for one kid in her class to say "Stop. She did the right thing." But nobody spoke up to defend her. So now, even though she knew she wasn't supposed to call attention to herself, Yuki had to say something.

A gasp came from the ladies behind the curtains and the screens. The gentlemen in the hall all turned to stare at her.

Yuki raised her fan to cover the lower part of her face and took a few steps toward Shōnagon.

"Your Majesty," Yuki said. "Nobu is just a kid, and sometimes kids make mistakes. He deserves a second chance. Please."

The emperor glowered. Yuki glanced uneasily at Shōnagon, who pressed her lips together and looked pale even beneath her powder.

"When somebody is guilty of a crime in the palace, the penalties are banishment or decapitation," the emperor said. "Those are the only choices."

Maybe because she had grown up as an only child, Yuki wasn't afraid to challenge adults. She remembered that her father used to say that to get what he wanted from the chair of his department, he had to appeal to the man's big ego. Could that work with an emperor, too?

"You're the emperor," Yuki said. "You can add a new choice. If you came up with a different punishment for Nobu and Okinamaro, then Shōnagon would write about this scene in her pillow book and you would be forever known for your wisdom and grace."

"Who are you?" the emperor demanded.

Yuki wasn't certain if he really wanted to know or if he was trying to put her in her place.

"Her name is Yuki, and she is from the Land of a Merry Cat," Shōnagon said.

"Might she also be the stranger in the most recent prophecy?"

Yuki turned to see a man in a boxy black tunic with a leaf pattern sweep into the hall, trailed by a group of aides. He had the craggy good looks of an aging movie star.

"Which prophecy are you referring to, Regent Fujiwara?" the emperor asked sullenly.

"When the master of divination looked for auspicious days for the Chinese delegation to visit, he foresaw a stranger who would offer wise counsel," the regent said.

"Yes, that's right!" the empress exclaimed. "And Yuki is correct. You can change the rules."

"Well then, stranger from a merry land, what would you suggest?" the emperor asked.

Yuki almost said, "It's 'Land of a Merry Cat,'" but caught herself in the nick of time. "When I do something wrong, my mother makes me do extra chores," she said.

"You could assign Nobu to the stables to clean up after the oxen," the empress suggested. "I suppose Okinamaro could be given a second chance as well. Perhaps he could go to the servants' quarters."

"That would be punishing the servants, not the dog," the regent observed.

"Page boy," the emperor said. "You are hereby demoted to work in the ox stables until the full moon. Okinamaro, you will stay in the servants' quarters, where there will be no crispy duck-skin treats or silk cushions for you. I hope you have both learned your lesson."

"Thank you, Your Royal Majesty," Nobu said, bowing deeply.

Okinamaro jumped up and barked, ears perked forward. As the guards released Nobu, he shot Yuki a dazed smile. She couldn't believe it. They had listened to her. Back home, nobody ever listened to her. Not her mother. Not Julio. Certainly not her English teacher. She felt her shoulders relax as she stood a little straighter. She liked this feeling of being an influencer. Already Shōnagon's world was way better than Santa Dolores.

"Yuki from the Land of a Merry Cat," the regent said, causing her heartbeat to spike. Though his voice was friendly, his smile was thin and hard. "Shōnagon, is this your contestant?"

"Yes," Shōnagon said. "She has just arrived from her long journey."

"We must alert the chamberlain and the master of divination at once to set the date for the contest," the regent said, clapping his hands together. "Is Lady Shikibu present?"

Yuki wanted to ask if he meant Murasaki Shikibu, author of *The Tale of Genji*. But she decided she'd drawn enough attention to herself for one day.

"Yes, I am here." A woman even shorter than Shōnagon stepped around the curtain where the consort had been seated. Murasaki had a narrow chin, deep-set eyes, and a reserved air.

"Ah, Murasaki," the regent said. "Is your contestant with you?"

"She is busy with her studies," Murasaki said. "Should I send for her?"

"No need to disturb her," the regent said. "Here are the

chamberlain and the master of divination. Gentlemen, the other contestant has arrived. I have called you to set a date for the contest."

The two men had gray hair and wispy beards that reached their knees. One wore a white robe with a large black circle on his chest. The black circle was covered in interconnected red dots. The other man wore a black robe with a white circle that also contained red dots. Each carried a large paper scroll.

"Master of divination, how long will it take you to determine the most auspicious day?" the regent asked the man in white.

"Regent Fujiwara, in anticipation of your request, I have already consulted the stars," said the master of divination.

"And I the emperor's schedule," said the one in black, who had to be the chamberlain.

"We have determined that the most auspicious time to begin the contest will be in two days during the Hour of the Dog," the master of divination said.

That meant the contest would be held on her birthday. Should she tell them? Given that Nobu had nearly lost his head, Yuki suspected nobody at court was going to care whether she wanted to compete on her birthday or not.

"Two days," the empress said with a gasp. "Should we not give Yuki some time to prepare?"

"I agree," Shōnagon said. "It would only be fair."

The emperor smirked. "Perhaps your contestant would be prepared if you had chosen one from the provinces instead of from a foreign land," he said.

"Even girls from the provinces require training," Shōnagon said. "As you heard from Murasaki, the other contestant is studying as we speak."

"The stars have given us the most auspicious time and we will abide by it," the regent said. "Of course, Shōnagon, it's quite understandable that you would be anxious, given that this might be your last contest."

Yuki looked at Shōnagon with confusion. What did the regent mean?

"Nonsense," Shōnagon said, though her smile was tight. "I relish the challenge."

"I, too, look forward to this final chapter," Murasaki said, the corner of her mouth turning upward ever so slightly.

Shōnagon shot her a withering look. "I promise you, this is far from over," she said.

"That's the spirit," the regent said. "Let the battle begin."

Yuki had the feeling that the imperial court was not all that different from middle school. There were the cool kids who everybody tried to impress and the bullies who everyone tried to appease. But the consequences felt more real here. More dangerous. And—if she was being honest with herself—more exciting.

After they left the emperor's quarters and returned to the empress's wing, Yuki was mobbed by the empress's ladies, who crowded around and peppered her with questions. "Does everyone in your country have a cat?" "Why are the cats merry?" "How many cats does your family have?" Since Yuki had been studying ancient Egypt in social studies, she told them that cats were revered in her country because they killed rats and snakes, and that when the cats died, they were mummified and buried with their families. Yes, everyone worked hard to keep their cats happy. And yes, she had two cats, named Pusheen and Nala—which was not entirely a lie, as she had Pusheen and Nala stuffed animals on her bed.

From there, the questions got harder. "How long did it take you to travel across the sea?" asked Lady Hyōbu.

"Oh, about seven days?" Yuki replied.

A little girl tugged on her sleeve. "How did you learn our language?"

"Everyone speaks at least three languages in the Land of a Merry Cat," Yuki told her. "English, Japanese, and the language of cats called Meow."

"How on earth did Shōnagon find you?" Lady Ukon asked.

At this last question, Izumi interjected, "That's enough, ladies. Yuki has much to do before the contest begins."

Izumi pulled her out to the veranda. "You better hope they don't bring you a cat to converse with," she muttered.

"If they do, I will tell them that the cat says it wants a treat and a nap and to be left alone," Yuki said.

Izumi set out a cushion next to Shōnagon for Yuki to sit on. Shōnagon was watching a team of gardeners add fresh snow to the mountain. They had leaned a ladder against the mountain and each gardener climbed to a different rung.

Then they passed a bucket of snow up the line. The gardener at the top tossed the snow onto the mountain and used a small board strapped to his hand to smooth the surface. Shōnagon appeared to be completely absorbed in watching the men toss and smooth the snow on the mountain.

Yuki fidgeted. "Why are we watching this?" she asked, mystified.

"Clear your mind for the moment," Shōnagon said. "See how the gardener who fills the bucket levels off the snow each time he refills it so that the amount is exact? When the one at the top smooths the surface, do you notice how precise his strokes are? I find that watching them helps me write. If you ever feel stuck during the contest, you should close your eyes and envision this. Words are buckets of snow that you are using to shape the mountain. Inspiration comes from repetition. As you gain experience, you will come to trust in this."

Yuki didn't quite understand how inspiration came from repetition. It sounded like a version of her mother's favorite saying, "Practice makes perfect," which had not helped her the year that she took piano lessons and blanked in the middle of her recital piece.

When a gardener wheeled away the empty cart, Shōnagon turned to look at Yuki with the same deliberate gaze she had fixed on the snow mountain. Yuki was convinced that Shōnagon could see deep inside her, to the thoughts swirling in her head and the blood pumping through her heart.

"You must be quite concerned over what happened in the

emperor's chamber," Shōnagon said.

"Is it normal for the emperor to sentence people to death for something small like that?" Yuki asked.

Shōnagon looked startled. "Death?" she said quizzically.

"He threatened to cut Nobu's head off," Yuki said.

"Ah, I see," Shōnagon said, nodding. "Here decapitation is a spell that removes all memories from your head. It is a form of death. But not actual death."

"Oh," Yuki said. Still. She was glad that she had come to Nobu's defense. Walking around like a zombie was not much of a life.

"Now, let us talk about the contest," Shōnagon said. "What will take place in two days is merely the opening ceremony. The three rounds of the contest will be held on subsequent days. Izumi and I will help you prepare for each round. Likewise, Murasaki Shikibu will be working with the consort's contestant."

"Is she the author of *The Tale of Genji*?" Yuki asked. She knew that Shōnagon and Murasaki were the most famous authors of their era. Her father had a copy of *The Tale of Genji* on his bookshelf. He had taken an interest in Japanese literature after meeting her mother. He might have had *The Pillow Book*, too. If only Yuki had thought to look in the boxes of books in the garage, she might have used his copy instead of going to the library. She always felt more connected to him when she listened to one of his albums or read one of his books.

"Yes, I have heard from previous contestants that Murasaki

is also quite famous," Shōnagon said with a stiff smile. "I have even heard that she has been deemed the more serious writer. But I don't mind. People say they enjoy my musings and I would much rather be interesting than serious."

Yuki had the feeling Shōnagon did mind very much, so she changed the subject. "Why did the regent say this might be your last contest?" she asked.

"If either Murasaki or I lose three contests in a row, we are to be decapitated and banished to the Tedium. Of course, after decapitation, being exiled hardly matters. Without her memories, a writer cannot write. I have lost the previous two contests. This is the first time that I have been on the brink of elimination."

"Why would he do that to you or Murasaki?" Yuki said, outraged. "You're two of the most famous writers from Japan."

"Let me tell you how the contest came to be and then I will answer your question," Shōnagon said. "A crack first appeared in the sky during the reign of our previous emperor."

Yuki was tempted to interrupt and tell Shōnagon that the sky was not solid but made up of gases, mostly nitrogen and oxygen. She could also explain why the sky was blue. But that would be her acting like a know-it-all, and Shōnagon probably wouldn't believe her anyway.

"Have you heard of Amaterasu?" Shōnagon asked.

Yuki nodded. "I've read about her in books," she said. "Amaterasu is the sun goddess and the most important goddess in Japan."

"That's correct," Shōnagon said. "Unfortunately, the previous emperor became very ill and, breaking centuries of tradition, began worshipping the moon god, Tsukuyomi. The moon god was once the husband of our great sun goddess, Amaterasu. Because of his violent temper, she had thrown him out of the heavens. Not surprisingly, this former emperor's decision to worship Tsukuyomi offended Amaterasu. That's when the crack appeared. The master of divination at the time sought guidance from the witches of Mount Osore, who told him that unless the sun goddess was appeased, the sky would shatter and plunge the world into darkness. He returned with a prophecy that instructed the court to find the best young poet in the land to serve as the high priestess of poetry, performing daily rites in the sun goddess's honor. Before the first contest could be held, the emperor who worshipped the moon god passed, and Emperor Ichijō took the throne. The regent decided to raise the level of intrigue by having the poets in the contest represent the consort and the empress, pitting the two retinues against each other. After the first priestess was named, the crack in the sky disappeared. But over time, as the priestess's creativity waned, the crack returned. When a new priestess was appointed, the crack faded once again. The contest typically takes place every fourth cycle of the moon."

Yuki couldn't imagine a more talented writer than Shōnagon. "Why does there need to be a contest? Can't you be the high priestess?"

Shōnagon hid an amused smile behind her sleeve. "I'm afraid I do not have the necessary qualifications, as I'm far too old and have already been married," she said. "The high priestess is always a girl in her twelfth or thirteenth year, and she must remain unmarried."

Yuki had no problem with that. Nobody had ever had a crush on her, anyway. Nobu was too good-looking to be interested in her.

"The regent also decided to tie my fate and Murasaki's to the contests," Shōnagon said. "I believe his true aim, besides entertaining the court with this game, is to build his daughter's reputation as the center of culture at court and push Empress Teishi aside. If I lose and Murasaki stays, that is to the consort's advantage. This is a pivotal contest for myself and for the empress."

"Wow," Yuki said. There was a lot riding on the outcome. She could single-handedly save Shōnagon and fix the sky. "Where do the high priestesses go once they're replaced?"

"Since the contest began, we have had eight high priestesses, and the previous seven have all chosen to remain at the temple," Shōnagon said. "They have their own literary salon."

That sounded pretty great, spending all day writing poetry with other poets. Forever was a long time, though. Yuki would miss her mother. And probably things like pizza and indoor plumbing. But Hana had Doug now and soon they would have a new baby. Her mother would be too busy to miss her. No way did Yuki want to go home to a screaming baby and poopy diapers.

"What about the losers?" Yuki asked. "What happens to them?"

"Alas, the losers do not get to stay," Shōnagon said. "So many questions! I suppose times have changed and girls have more opportunities. Until now, our contestants have been simply desperate to win and have a position at court."

Even if Yuki lost, this would be an adventure. Since she didn't have paper and a pen, she made a list of pros and cons in her head.

Pro: Being trained by the great writer Sei Shōnagon for the poetry contest.

Con: Living in a land run by a power-hungry regent and a weak emperor.

Pro: Getting back at my mother for ruining my life.

Con: Feeling bad about making her worry.

Pro: Never going back to Juana Maria Middle School if I win.

Con: None of the kids will know what a big deal I am in the imperial court.

Pro: Never hearing another silly Doug joke.

Yuki turned to Shōnagon. "I want to be the next high priestess," she said. "I'll compete in the contest."

"How outstandingly splendid," Shōnagon said. Though it occurred to Yuki that she might have been referring to the snow mountain.

That evening, the empress presented Yuki with gifts, a stack of silk robes and a wood box filled with fans and hair ornaments. The air in the empress's quarters was festive. Twangy, atonal string and flute music floated in from the garden while the two ladies sitting next to her gossiped about the musicians.

"You see the gentleman playing the flute?" said Lady Ukon. "He has a very high opinion of himself. Yet he can't recognize the lines to the most common poems."

"And his calligraphy!" Lady Nijō said. "Atrocious."

"The gentleman on the thirteen-string zither smells like spring rain," Lady Ukon said.

"But his head is in the clouds," Lady Nijō said. "Once he mistook a sideboard in the emperor's dining room for a shoe rack and left his shoes there. Ugh. Can you imagine?"

Yuki used to shake her head when the girls made cootie catchers to determine who they would marry and how many kids they would have and where they would live. Yet now she was fascinated hearing about which gentlemen had sloppy handwriting and which ones smelled good. She loved that the ladies didn't treat her like a little kid.

When a messenger knocked, Izumi rose to answer the door. She returned with a piece of paper that had been folded into a skinny strip with a knot tied in the middle. A sprig of delicate pink flowers had been slipped into the knot.

"Lady Hyōbu has a letter," Izumi said. "Come with me to deliver it."

Yuki got to her feet. She hadn't decided if she liked Izumi or not. But she thought it was a good sign that Izumi wanted her company. "What kind of flower is that?" she asked.

"This is the bush clover," Izumi said. "I suspect the letter is from a gentleman."

They found Lady Hyōbu and Shōnagon behind a screen playing go, a board game with black and white stones that reminded Yuki of a very complicated game of checkers. Lady Hyōbu unfolded the letter with excitement. At the sight of the bush clover, Shōnagon gave her a knowing smile.

"Ah, he misses you," she said.

"I have not heard from him in some time," Lady Hyōbu said. "Izumi, could you fetch my writing box?"

Izumi returned with a black-lacquered box with gold bamboo stalks on the lid. Inside was a dark, smooth stone about the size of a spoon rest. Izumi showed Yuki how to wet the stone with water and then grind a rectangular black ink stick in circles against the surface. When the ink was the right consistency, not too thick or thin, Izumi told Yuki to use the ink stick to sweep the black liquid into two divots at the top of the stone. Making the ink felt satisfying and purposeful.

Lady Hyōbu wrote her response, then turned the paper toward Shōnagon. "What do you think?" she asked.

"The bellflower is a confident choice," Shōnagon said. "Where is Nobu? Ah, I forgot. He almost lost his head and now he's in the stable because of that silly dog. Izumi, can you find a bellflower in the garden?"

Yuki accompanied Izumi, clattering down the stairs in a pair of high wooden clogs. The sun had gone down and the stars gleamed in the indigo sky. As they walked along the garden path, fireflies winked in the bushes and cicadas whirred in the trees.

"I wish people in my time wrote letters like yours," Yuki said. "It's so sophisticated."

"What are your letters like?" Izumi asked.

"Well, we don't write letters on paper very often," Yuki said. "Most people compose messages to each other on what's called a cell phone. It's a little machine that fits in your hand."

Izumi frowned. "What is a machine?"

Right, they didn't have machines yet. "A machine is like a tool, I guess," Yuki said. "This tool helps you write messages. Let's say I was the high priestess at the temple. Instead of sending you a letter by messenger, you'd get my note immediately on your phone, and you could write me back from the palace."

"Half the fun of writing a letter is choosing the paper," Izumi said.

"I like writing letters on paper better, too," Yuki agreed. "Also, we don't attach flowers to our letters like you do. Instead, we would put a picture of a flower in our message. We could also play games together on the same machine. We could see each other's moves in the area where you write messages."

"You must have a very powerful master of divination to send words and games through the air," Izumi said.

"We have two," Yuki said. "Their names are Apple and Android."

After they crossed a low stone bridge over a stream, Izumi said they had entered the autumn quadrant, where they would find the bellflower. They passed beneath trees with red, orange, and yellow leaves. Bush clover cascaded down a trellis.

"Izumi, how many of Shōnagon's contestants have you trained?" Yuki asked.

"Oh, all of them, of course," Izumi said. "You're the ninth."

"Right," Yuki said. "I was thinking about how in my world about a hundred years pass between contests. That's a long time in my world. How much time passes for you?"

"So far the contest has been held every summer, or every fourth cycle of the moon," Izumi said.

"When you say moon cycle, do you mean from new moon to new moon?" Yuki asked.

"Yes," Izumi said. "This moon cycle is summer. The next will be autumn. And so on."

Yuki frowned as she worked this out. That meant four lunar months here equaled one hundred years back home. Izumi suddenly grabbed Yuki's sleeve and pulled her behind a tree. Peeking around the trunk, Izumi gestured toward the stairs of the consort's quarters. Yuki peered over her and saw someone hurrying down the steps into the garden.

"I think that's the other contestant," Izumi whispered.

"What makes you think that?" Yuki whispered back.

"Because she walks funny," Izumi said.

The girl did seem to fight her robes rather than flow with them. As they hurried to follow her, sweat trickled down

Yuki's forehead from the effort.

"These robes are so heavy," Yuki said. "It's like walking around in a wet blanket. Do you think she's from my time, too?"

"Not necessarily," Izumi said. "The girls from the provinces aren't accustomed to dressing up like we do in the capital, either."

Izumi's dismissive tone made it clear she thought the girls from the provinces were inferior to girls in the capital. The girls from the provinces hadn't had the same opportunities, though. Not having fancy clothes didn't make them less smart or less worthy.

"That's one nice thing about my time," Yuki said. "The pants that I had on when I first got here? Those are called jeans and everyone wears them, rich or poor."

Izumi smirked. "No letters and ugly clothes," she said. "I should never want to visit you in your world."

"You might like Victorian England, then," Yuki said tartly.

They hurried around a bend in the path, staying in the shadows. When the path straightened out, Izumi grabbed Yuki's arm again and they froze. The girl had stopped beneath an arbor and was crouching on the ground with her back to them. A strange glow that did not come from fireflies or the moon seemed to emanate from her. Yuki heard a hiccupy sound. At first, she thought she was hearing a frog or a cricket. Then she realized the other contestant was crying.

When Yuki took a step toward the girl, Izumi tightened her grip on her arm.

"I think we should go," Izumi whispered. "She could be a fox."

"What do you mean? She's clearly a girl," Yuki said, confused.

"Foxes like to play tricks at night by shapeshifting into humans and pretending that they need help," Izumi said.

That had to be a silly superstition. Then again, if the girl did turn out to be a fox, Yuki would know for sure that she had entered an alternate dimension.

"Are you all right?" Yuki called out.

The glow disappeared. The girl scrambled to her feet and backed away from them. But her stance relaxed once she saw they were kids her own age.

"I'm fine. I dropped something, that's all," the girl said. Her eyes looked watery, though, and her face powder had streaks as if she had wiped away tears.

"I'm Yuki," she said. "I'm here for the contest. What's your name?"

"That makes us competitors, then," the girl said. "I'm Jun."

Yuki studied Jun, who had put her outer robe on over her hair, hiding its length. It occurred to Yuki that if Jun had pierced ears, she was probably from the twenty-first century, too. But in the dark, Yuki couldn't see whether Jun had the telltale dots on her earlobes or not.

"Where are you from?" Izumi asked.

"The provinces," Jun said, a shade too quickly.

"Of course," Izumi said. "Which one?"

"I'm from . . ." Jun paused and a guarded look entered

85

her eyes. "Etch—Echizen. You know what? I shouldn't be talking to you. I should go."

Yuki stepped to the side as Jun pushed past her and hurried away.

"Well, she's definitely a person and not a fox," Yuki said. "Is whatever she said a real province?"

"It is," Izumi said, watching Jun leave through narrowed eyes. "Echizen is also where Murasaki lived for a year. Her father was posted there. What do you think that strange light was?"

"I have no idea," Yuki said.

Yuki and Izumi continued their search for the bellflower. When they found the star-shaped purple blossom, Izumi gave her a mini lecture about its importance as one of the seven autumn flowers in poetry. Yuki suspected that she would not remember half of what Izumi said by morning. What she would always remember about the bellflower was a girl crying in the moonlight.

6

Things That Make the Heart Beat Faster

Yuki studied each striped shell in the circle, trying to soften her eyes as Shōnagon had instructed. She was looking for a match with eight stripes. But the lines on some shells were so faint, she couldn't be sure. They'd been playing a matching game called *kai-awase* all morning, where each player took turns finding the mate to the shell in the center of the circle. The shell interiors had been painted with birds, flowers, trees, and other things from nature. Once a match was made, the player came up with a poem on the spot based on the painting. But Yuki was having a hard time making a match, much less a poem.

Holding the center shell in her palm, she chose a second shell at random and tried to put the two sides together inside her sleeve. The shells skidded apart.

Yuki sighed with disappointment. "Not a match," she said, returning them to their original spots.

With her sleeve hiding her hand, Shōnagon picked up two shells. Yuki heard the telltale click. Then Shōnagon held up the two shells to show the interiors, each painted with orange flowers. In a poem-reciting voice, she said, "The scent of the tiger lily wafts on the summer breeze. If only I had something to remember you by besides these wild blooms."

Yuki's shoulders slumped. "Maybe we should stop playing and just work on the poems," she said.

"That is the easier part," Shōnagon said. "In the contest, I will always supply you with the first line and all you have to do is build on it." She took a new shell out of a lacquered canister and set it in the center of the circle. "Go again," she said.

As Yuki bent over to get a closer look, Izumi came in and inspected the large collection of shells that Shōnagon had amassed. Then her gaze shifted to the one match Yuki had discovered, purely by luck. "Well, this seems to be going well," Izumi said.

"How observant of you," Yuki said tartly.

"I'm only stating the facts," Izumi said.

"Let's take a break," Shōnagon said, rising. "Izumi, come with me to visit the mistress of the wardrobe about our outfits for the contest."

After they left, Yuki went to the floor-to-ceiling woven blind that separated the study in the empress's quarters from the veranda. Pulling back the blind, she looked at the garden. Now that she had spent hours hearing Shōnagon come up with poems from the images painted inside the shells, she realized what Izumi meant by the garden's quadrants. To the right was spring, where cherry trees and hot-pink azaleas bloomed. To the left, where the fireflies had been, she spotted summer flowers like lavender and hydrangea. Autumn leaves blazed in the far left corner where she and Izumi had cut the sprig of bellflower. That meant the far right corner, which was not colorful or showy from this distance, had to be winter. For the first time since she had arrived, Yuki felt like she was looking at something that made sense to her.

Near an arbor in the center, a white ball arcing in the air caught her eye. Anybody could be playing with the ball. Yet Yuki found herself hoping the mystery player was Nobu. Since she was on a break, she might as well take a walk and see. At the bottom of the stairs, Yuki touched her hair. Was she a frizzy mess? If she went all the way back to Shōnagon's room to check, she might miss her opportunity to see Nobu. She kept going toward the arbor.

Following the path that cut between spring and summer, she passed tulips and peonies on her right, sunflowers and star lilies on her left. Now that she was inside the garden, she could hear but no longer see the ball being kicked. When she reached the arbor, covered in long wispy wisteria vines, she looked around. Where had the ball player gone?

Then she heard a rustling overhead. Taking a step back, she spotted Nobu crawling on top of the arbor, trying to knock the ball loose.

When the ball bounced to the ground, she grabbed it. Nobu dropped down from the arbor, blanching as he saw her.

"My ball got stuck," he said. "Please don't tell anyone that you saw me up there."

"I don't know," she said, tossing the ball back to him. "What's in it for me? I already saved your head once."

He grinned, kicking the ball repeatedly straight up into the air. She noticed that he had a chipped front tooth. This small flaw somehow made him more appealing.

"Thank you for speaking up," he said. "That was very brave."

"It was the right thing to do," she said with a shrug.

"Oh, sorry," he said as the ball sailed toward her.

She stuck out her foot and the ball bounced off her ankle. Or through the layers of robe around her ankle, anyway. He gaped at her as the ball whipped past him into the bushes.

"Nice kick," he said, chasing after the ball.

"We have a game called soccer where you kick the ball and don't touch it with your hands," she said. "But in soccer the ball mostly stays on the ground."

"Like this?" He rolled the ball toward her.

She stopped the ball with her foot and kicked it back to him. "Like that," she said, as they continued to tap the ball back and forth. "So is it hard work, being in the stable?"

"I don't mind it," Nobu said. "Oxen are far less demanding than the courtiers, though I do miss being in the palace. How are your studies?"

"This morning I had a crash course in *kai-awase*," Yuki said. "I'm terrible at it."

Nobu raised his eyebrows. "What is a course that crashes? Did you break the shells?"

"No, that's a saying in my country," Yuki said. "A crash course is when you have to learn how to do something new quickly. Like maybe you had a crash course in how to hitch an ox."

"I see," he said with amusement. "I did receive instructions. But there were no loud noises and I managed not to run into anything."

"That's good," she said. She couldn't believe that she was talking to a boy not named Julio and she wasn't making an idiot of herself. "The problem I'm having with *kai-awase* is finding the match. The shell patterns all look the same to me."

"Well, I have only watched the ladies play," he said. "I think the best players focus on joining two shells rather than matching them, if that makes sense."

Joining and not matching. She didn't know exactly what he meant. But she didn't want to hurt his feelings. "Kind of," Yuki said.

"There you are," Izumi said, hurrying up to them with an exasperated look. "Oh, hello, Nobu. I hear you've found your intellectual peers in the stable."

Nobu picked up the ball and rested it against his hip. "It's true, oxen are humble beasts," he said. "But at least they do not put on airs. Good luck with the *kai-awase*, Yuki."

Nobu left in the direction of the winter garden. As Yuki strolled alongside Izumi, she wondered why Izumi had acted like such a snob toward Nobu. Was it possible that Izumi had a crush on him?

"What was that all about?" Yuki asked. "You weren't very nice."

"When you've lived in the palace long enough, you see boys getting promoted because they are liked," Izumi said. "Everybody likes Nobu. He will probably rise to be a minister one day. Meanwhile, we girls must have exquisite handwriting, impressive talent on a musical instrument, and a superior knowledge of poetry. Yet we gain nothing from our efforts. It's all so that we can be married off into the right family."

"That is unfair," Yuki agreed. "That is one thing that is better in my world. Girls can go to school and have careers, and they only get married if they want to."

"All I want to do is read and write poetry," Izumi said. "I don't want to be my mother."

"I understand more than you know," Yuki said.

Back in the study, Shōnagon laid out another set of shells, and this time Yuki followed Nobu's advice. She stopped trying to count the number of stripes on each. Instead, she tried to take in the slight differences, the hue from one shell to the next, the shape of the bump at the hinge, the overall topography. She got better at figuring out which two shells went together. Nothing was more satisfying than the click of a shell finding its mate.

"Now that you have a feel for the shells, we can discuss strategy for the poems," Shōnagon said. "The key is that you and I must always agree. Your line must build on mine. The easiest way is for you to supply the emotion behind the image. For example, if I say, 'Deep in the mountains, the lonely pine waits for signs of spring,' what might your line be?"

Yuki went blank, her mind filling with white static, a paralyzing blizzard of nothingness. She closed her eyes. The blizzard turned into a mountain of snow that she shaped and smoothed with her own hands. "While memories of you linger in the branches," she said.

"Yes," Shōnagon said, her voice rising with excitement. "Yes, that is exactly right."

Yuki thought *kai-awase* could be a distant cousin to the *Pitch Perfect* riff-off. The matching shells chose the category and then the contestant riffed off their partner's opening line. Yuki recited poems about bamboo and tiger lilies and cypress trees bending in the wind, about pine trees and camellias and egrets standing in a lotus pond. In their last game of the day, Yuki beat Shōnagon.

"Have you been bewitched by a fox?" Shōnagon exclaimed. "You can't be the same girl who played *kai-awase* this morning."

Yuki felt her heart swell with pride. She had no talent for

sports or art or music. She didn't know how to style her hair or do her makeup or alter her clothes in a way that made kids notice her and think she was cool. But here she was good at something that other people respected. Here they admired her. She felt destined to be high priestess.

Yet as darkness fell, Yuki began to feel out of sorts. Seeing an attendant pull her little girl into her lap reminded Yuki of her own mother, who had to be frantic. The thought made Yuki giddy and a little queasy at the same time. Part of her wanted to get back at Hana, to show her how it felt to be abandoned. Until Doug came along, they had done everything together. Then suddenly every outing, every take-out order, and every TV binge-watch had to involve Doug. Yuki understood that he was part of their lives. But did he have to be part of every minute of every day?

Sitting on the veranda, she snacked on a bowl of berries and watched the fireflies wink in the garden. The skimpy dinner of fish and pickled vegetables had left her craving a giant plate of pasta with fake parmesan cheese that came out of a green Kraft can. And she was dying to get her hair off her neck and pull it into a high ponytail.

"Hello," a whispery voice said, causing Yuki to jump.

Yuki looked around the veranda but didn't see anyone. "Hello?" she said.

"I'm right here."

Yuki looked down to her right and gasped. The golden pheasant stood next to her, cocking its golden head, which resembled a pharaoh's headdress.

"You can talk," Yuki said. She knew parrots could repeat words. But she was not aware of any birds that knew how to have a conversation.

"If there is someone worth talking to," the pheasant said.

Yuki was pretty sure that's what the flowers had said to Alice. Maybe this was all a dream, then. "How did you learn to speak?" she asked.

"When you are in a cage all the time, you have no choice but to listen to people," the pheasant said.

"That makes sense," Yuki said. "Do all the animals talk here? Can Okinamaro talk?"

"Don't be silly," the pheasant said. "But the dog is useful, as it knows how to open my cage."

"Who else do you talk to in the palace?" Yuki asked.

"Very few humans can hear me," the pheasant said. "Shōnagon's first visitor taught me many words. But then she went away. The others got scared when I spoke to them."

"Now *you're* being silly," Yuki said. "There's nothing scary about you."

"They think they must be going mad, that's why," the pheasant said.

"That didn't cross my mind, but maybe it should have," Yuki said. "I know the empress misses you. Should I take you to her?"

"I do not miss the empress," the bird said. "She keeps me in a cage."

95

"Well, I won't tell her that I saw you, then," Yuki said. "You shouldn't be in a cage. You should be free." She slid her bowl closer to the bird. "Do pheasants like berries?"

The pheasant's eyes widened. "I have not had berries since I lived in the wild," the bird said.

Yuki smiled as the pheasant snatched up the berries in its beak and gulped them down.

"You have been very kind," the pheasant said. "I would not like the fate of the others to fall on you. Please beware of the scrolling."

"What's the scrolling?" Yuki asked.

"The thing you should beware of," the pheasant said. Then the bird flapped its wings and fluttered into the garden.

"Wait!" Yuki called out, jumping to her feet. A maid carrying a tray came around the corner and shot her a puzzled look. Probably the maid thought Yuki had been talking to herself.

Making her way back to Shōnagon's room, Yuki mulled the pheasant's warning. In the Looking-Glass world, words sometimes had no meaning at all, like when Alice rode in a boat with the sheep who kept shouting "Feather!" Maybe what the pheasant said about the scrolling was like that. Maybe it was random and absurd and there was no deeper meaning to understand.

Yuki's hand hovered over the center shell. The beige lines on the potential matches wavered and then went haywire before her eyes, like a polygraph test when the suspect on a detective show told a lie. She didn't know how she was supposed to make a match with the lines moving like this. As suddenly as the wild swings began, they slowed, and the lines settled. Yuki noticed a thick band across the center shell. She quickly found the match and heard the click inside her sleeve. Then she presented the interiors to the blurry faces in the audience.

"Not a match," said a high whispery voice. The golden pheasant came into focus on the other side of the *kai-awase* circle.

Shocked, Yuki looked at the painted interiors. One showed a purple iris, the other a pink cherry blossom. "But I heard the click," she said.

The pheasant blinked its wide eyes. "Not a match," the bird said. "When are you going to wake up?"

Yuki's eyes popped open. She lay on a thin woven mat on the floor facing the dark wood shutters. Sunlight seeped through the gaps in the latticed shutters. Disoriented, she rolled over to find Izumi lounging on the floor next to her and leafing through a thick book that kicked up dust with every flip of the page.

"Finally," Izumi said. "I was starting to think you were going to sleep all day."

Yuki sat up and pushed aside the silk robe that she'd used as a bedcover. Her back felt stiff from sleeping on the floor. "I just had the strangest dream," she said. "I was playing *kai-awase* and the golden pheasant kept saying, 'Not a match.'"

"The empress's golden pheasant?" Izumi burst out laughing. "At least the pheasant did me the courtesy of waking you. We have so much work to do."

Had Yuki imagined the pheasant talking to her the night before? It didn't seem real now. What if she'd had an accident on her bike on the way to Momo's store and was lying unconscious in a hospital bed dreaming this?

"What, you've never heard the golden pheasant speak?" Yuki said in a joking tone.

"Uh, no," Izumi said. "Why, do pheasants talk in the Land of a Merry Cat?"

Yuki debated whether to tell Izumi about the pheasant's warning. Given that Okinamaro had almost been sent to the Tedium for a minor offense, what would happen to the pheasant if the regent found out the bird was warning visitors about the contest? Yuki thought the bird had a good heart and she didn't want to be responsible for anything happening to the pheasant.

"That's hard to say, since they're hiding from the cats," Yuki said.

While Yuki got dressed and combed her hair, Izumi went to the writing box on the desk and made ink.

"Today I'm going to read you poems so that you get a feel for the rhythms," Izumi said. "I find it works best if you write down the line and repeat it back to me."

Izumi moved over to make room for Yuki at the desk and

scanned the poetry anthology. Yuki took a piece of paper from the stack next to the writing box and picked up a brush.

"Here's a good one," Izumi said. "'Were it not for the song of the mountain thrush rising through the glen.'"

Yuki worried that she would make a mess with the brush and dribble ink everywhere. But the brush seemed to guide her hand. She scribbled the line, reciting as she wrote: "'Were it not for the song of the mountain thrush in the glen.'"

"Listen carefully," Izumi said. "'Rising through the glen.'"

"'Rising through the glen,'" Yuki said.

"'Who would even suspect that spring has at long last arrived?'" Izumi continued.

Once Yuki had repeated the line, Izumi added, "You'll want to pay attention to seasons and the passage of time. The judges will look upon that favorably."

Izumi was a relentless teacher. If Yuki accidentally switched "a" with "the," Izumi made her repeat the line until she had it exactly right. After spending all morning on this exercise, Yuki's fingers were cramped from holding the brush and her throat was raw from reciting poems.

"Can we take a break?" Yuki asked.

Izumi looked at Yuki as if she'd sprouted a third eye. "The *kai-awase* round is tomorrow," Izumi said. "You can take a break when it's over."

Yuki set down her brush in protest. She was the super-nerd who loved school and was always complaining that her classmates let her do all the work. But Izumi was outnerding her. That's the kind of friend Yuki had needed back home—someone who made Yuki seem like the relaxed, easygoing one.

"It's a stupid rule that the contestants have to be from outside the capital," Yuki said. "You're the one who should be in the contest. It doesn't make sense to train me when you know so much."

Izumi threw up her hands. "Finally!" she exclaimed. "Thank you. You're the first contestant to ever say that. Of course, who doesn't want to improve their station in life? I understand why you're willing to compete for a high position at court. But have some perspective."

And then Yuki understood why Izumi had been so prickly. Izumi was better at poetry than any of the contestants, yet she couldn't compete. Yuki would feel the same way in her shoes.

"It's my deepest wish, to be the high priestess," Izumi admitted. "But Shōnagon says it's better to bring contestants through the mirror because you don't have any family here in our world. But the truth is, I hardly remember my family, since I spend all my time working at the palace."

"I'm sorry you can't compete," Yuki said. "If I win, can you come visit me at the temple?"

Izumi beamed. "Yes, I would love to visit," she said. "You must promise, though. Our last winning contestant said she would invite me and then I never heard from her."

"I promise on this book of poetry," Yuki said, setting her hand on top of the open tome.

Izumi also set her hand on the anthology. "And I promise to do everything in my power to help you win," she said.

They both laughed. Yuki thought her father would be proud of her. She was figuring out how to make new friends.

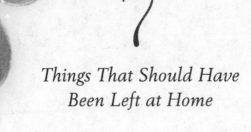

7

*Things That Should Have
Been Left at Home*

By the time Shōnagon entered the room with two maids in her wake, Yuki was surrounded by stacks of scribbled poems. Floral perfume wafted from the robes that the maids carried.

"It is so stiflingly hot in here," Shōnagon said. "Why haven't you opened the shutters? This room is hotter than the Eight Great Hells."

The maids set down the robes and dealt with the shutters. Izumi looked up from the poetry anthology. "Is it time to get dressed for the opening ceremony already?" she asked.

"Best to get started now," Shōnagon said. "Yuki's face is going to need a lot of work. Especially her eyebrows."

Izumi and Shōnagon had plucked theirs to oblivion and replaced them with black smudges, which reminded Yuki of the character No-Face in *Spirited Away*. Though she wanted to fit in here, she didn't want to look like a ghost clown.

"Eyebrows serve a purpose, you know," Yuki said. "They keep sweat and dirt out of your eyes. I think I should keep my eyebrows the way they are. That's the fashion in the Land of a Merry Cat."

"Remember, you are representing our empress, not yourself," Shōnagon said. "Also, you want the judges to focus on your poetry. If they are distracted by the caterpillars on your forehead, how do you think that will go?"

"Fine," Yuki said with a sigh.

Moving to the stool by the vanity, Yuki grimaced and tried not to flinch as Izumi yanked each eyebrow hair until only a thin line remained. After she had painted Yuki's face white, Izumi added the black smudges where her eyebrows had been and dark red color to her lips. Then Yuki watched in the mirror as Izumi combed out her hair with rice water to make it shine. One by one, Shōnagon handed Izumi the robes in the order she wanted them layered, a mix of greens and reds with a diamond-patterned red robe on top. Between the stark makeup and the bulky robes, Yuki didn't recognize herself in the mirror. The person in the reflection looked otherworldly and much older than almost-thirteen. Wait, not almost-thirteen. Thirteen! Today was her birthday. She'd been so busy studying that she forgot. Was Julio out celebrating with his new BFF Suzie? Had Yuki's mother even noticed that she was gone? It didn't matter now. Yuki had more important things to do than eat cake.

When they left for the empress's quarters, Yuki stuck close to Shōnagon, who also wore robes in reds and greens. She felt like Cinderella transformed for the ball, if the pumpkin carriage had taken a wrong turn and dropped her off at the Japanese imperial court instead. The empress's ladies bustled around and spoke in excited tones. "Has anyone seen my clogs?" called out a young girl. "Oh, look—I grabbed last summer's fan!" exclaimed an attendant. "Lady Hyōbu, please let me fix your train," a maid said. Outside, the setting sun turned the snow mountain into an orange and raspberry swirl.

"How delightfully festive," Shōnagon said. "I do love it when everyone is chasing flowers and butterflies."

"There are butterflies in here?" Yuki asked, looking around.

Shōnagon laughed merrily. "That would be lovely," she said. "However, it is only a figure of speech."

As Shōnagon made the rounds, Yuki tried to copy her smooth gait and air of self-assurance. She marveled at how Shōnagon always seemed to know exactly what to say. "Look at the way your hair cascades over your shoulders," Shōnagon exclaimed to one lady. She also exchanged poetic lines that doubled as inside jokes. "Suddenly we hear the lute's voice on the water," Shōnagon said archly to Lady Hyōbu, who giggled behind her sleeve. Though Yuki didn't know what the allusion meant, she hung on to Shōnagon's every word. When Empress Teishi emerged from her inner chambers in a plum robe with a flower pattern, Shōnagon declared her "magnificent" without sounding insincere or fawning.

"Yuki, I hear you've become a master at *kai-awase*," Empress Teishi said. "That's very impressive in such a short time!"

"I've had a great teacher," Yuki said, dazzled by the empress's radiance. If only the kids in Santa Dolores could see her now. In this world, the empress was not only talking to her, but giving her compliments.

As they lined up at the top of the stairs for the opening ceremony, Yuki looked down at the garden. The ceremony would take place on a stage in front of the lotus pond with the snow mountain as a backdrop. Directly across from the stage was a canopied platform for Emperor Ichijō. Gentlemen had already gathered in the courtyard, while ladies lined the verandas. Yuki spotted the regent near the emperor's platform and heard his deep, rumbling laugh.

When the flutists began to play, the master of divination, the chamberlain, and a minister who Yuki had not seen before filed into the garden and knelt on the stage. The consort and her attendants entered next and sat beneath a canopy between the stage and the emperor's dais. The consort was soft and plump and had a saucy air about her. Murasaki, who somehow managed to look modest yet haughty at the same time, knelt next to her. On Murasaki's other side was Jun, who had her hair pulled back into a low ponytail at the nape of her neck.

Prompted by some invisible cue, Shōnagon and Izumi herded her into line. Yuki followed them down the stairs to a canopy to the left of the stage. Shōnagon knelt next to Empress Teishi. Izumi directed Yuki to sit next to Shōnagon. The rest of the empress's entourage settled around them. When Emperor Ichijō had entered the garden and settled on his dais, the flutes dwindled. The master of divination stood to address the audience. In the pause, fans snapped open and closed and a low murmur of conversation ran through the crowd.

"Welcome, everyone, to the ninth cycle in our contest to name the high priestess of poetry," the master of divination said. "Look at these serious faces! While naming a new high priestess is indeed a very serious matter, it is also a joyous occasion. What an honor it is to witness the talents of two young poets vying to serve our great sun goddess, Amaterasu."

"Perhaps you can lighten the mood with one of the jokes or riddles you posed to me earlier," suggested the chamberlain.

"If you insist, my dear chamberlain," the master of divination said. "Why did the ox cross the road?"

The chamberlain tugged on his beard. "I still haven't the slightest idea," he said.

"Because the grass looked greener on the other side," the master of divination said, laughing at his own joke.

The minister serving as the third judge lifted his fan to hide a smirk. The audience groaned. Yuki couldn't believe it. She couldn't escape Doug jokes, even here.

"Here's one more," the master of divination said. "What has six legs but moves on four?"

"That would be a strange insect indeed," the chamberlain said.

"Oh, it's not an insect," the master of divination said. "The answer is a rider on horseback."

The chamberlain chuckled. "Oh, that's a good one," he said.

"Get on with the ceremony!" a courtier called out from the crowd.

"All right, all right," the master of divination said, waving his hand. "I must save the rest for our next moon-viewing party, anyway. Now I will introduce our contestants. Competing for Consort Shōshi is Jun from Echizen Province. And competing for Empress Teishi is Yuki from the Land of a Merry Cat, our first foreign contestant."

A murmur of surprise rippled through the audience. Yuki squirmed, feeling their eyes on her.

"Yes, it's quite a bold move by Empress Teishi!" the master of divination exclaimed. "Tomorrow night on this very stage, these young ladies will engage in *kai-awase*, testing both their powers of observation and their poetic talents. Lady Shikibu and Lady Shōnagon, who have been working with our young poets, need no introduction."

Shōnagon rose and Yuki followed her lead. Murasaki and Jun also stood up, and they all bowed to each other.

"May the best poet win," the master of divination said. "Until tomorrow, then."

When the flute music started up again, the emperor and his aides filed up the stairs to his quarters. Then Empress Teishi rose to leave.

"That's it?" Yuki whispered to Shōnagon as they returned to the empress's rooms.

"Oh yes, the opening ceremony is simply an excuse for a party," Shōnagon said.

Within minutes, servants arrived with fruit and wine. The ladies gossiped in groups with their robes swirling around them. Yuki thought they must look like flower petals from above. Meanwhile, messengers shuttled back and forth with messages for the ladies. When a letter arrived for Shōnagon, Yuki accompanied Izumi to deliver it to her. They found her talking in low tones to the empress. Izumi waited behind a screen until she was sure they could approach.

"She is ready, isn't she, Shōnagon?" Yuki overheard the empress say. "The emperor has been requesting the company of the consort more often than mine of late. My cousin seems to be winning his favor. I can't have my standing damaged further by a poor performance. I cannot fathom why you would pick a foreigner as our contestant. Was there truly no other choice?"

Once, at recess, Yuki had been hit so hard on the side of the head with a stray soccer ball that her mother took her to the ER to make sure she didn't have a concussion. The empress's words felt like that, which meant her encouragement before the ceremony had all been fake. She would probably be even more horrified if she knew that Yuki came from another century.

"The emperor calling for the consort may very well be the regent's doing," Shōnagon said in a soothing tone. "The regent wants you to worry, and to react either with anger or with sullenness toward the emperor. Your uncle is trying to place a chill on your relationship. This is why you must keep your head high and exude confidence. Try not to worry. Yuki will be a most outstanding contestant."

Shōnagon defending her did little to boost Yuki's mood. Yuki's distress must have been all over her face, because Izumi led her away without delivering the letter to Shōnagon. Instead, Izumi handed off the note to Lady Hyōbu and then found a quiet spot farther down the gallery. Izumi knelt with her apron-like train fanned out behind her. The rowdy voices of the courtiers singing drinking songs drifted through the garden.

"I just realized the empress is like the popular girls at my school," Yuki said. "Nice to your face and not nice behind your back."

"It's not you," Izumi said. "The empress always gets nervous the night before the contest. She questions the readiness of every contestant."

"I question my own readiness, so she's not alone," Yuki said glumly.

"The contests are unpredictable," Izumi said. "You can write an excellent poem, but the judges might like one specific thing the other poet did."

That was the problem with writing. It wasn't like running a race where the fastest person won. In elementary school, Yuki had been excited to work on the fifth-grade book about an endangered tiger named Trudy that would be sold to parents to raise money for endangered species. But when the tiger book came out, Yuki found her contributions had been limited to three paragraphs containing boring facts and data. She was the best writer in her grade! How had the teacher passed over her dramatic scene when the injured tiger was rescued? When Yuki went to the teacher in tears, he looked miffed as he explained the challenge of having to include every fifth grader in the text. Yuki hoped the contest judges would be fair.

"Did you like going to school?" Izumi asked.

"I liked the learning part," Yuki said. "I didn't always like dealing with the other kids."

"I would like to study Chinese, but only boys are allowed," Izumi said. "There is a rumor that Murasaki knows Chinese and that she learned it by eavesdropping on her brother's lessons. How long do girls go to school in the Land of a Merry Cat?"

"Everyone is supposed to go until they're around eighteen," Yuki said. "Then you can go to college if you want and focus on one subject. Like I'll probably get a degree in literature."

"I think I wouldn't mind traveling to your world if I could

go to college," Izumi said. "Even if I had to wear ugly pants."

Yuki laughed. "If I win, you come with me to the temple," she said. "And if I lose, you come with me through the mirror to the twenty-first century and go to school."

"I like that plan," Izumi said wistfully. She said it the way some kids wish for the pony they're never going to get.

"Do you want to take a walk in the garden?" Yuki asked. "I need some air."

"That's a good idea," Izumi said. "I can quiz you on plants and flowers."

"Great," Yuki said without enthusiasm.

They found their clogs and entered the garden by the now-familiar path that ran between spring and summer.

Izumi scanned the summer side of the path. "Let's start with the purple iris," she said. "Do you remember any of the poems we reviewed?"

Up ahead, Yuki saw the strange glow that had illuminated Jun. She raised her index finger to her lips and then pointed toward the light. Izumi nodded. When they reached the arbor, Izumi yelped with fright while Yuki guffawed. Jun was holding a phone.

Startled, Jun bobbled the device, which fell to the ground. Scooping up the phone, she wiped off the screen with her sleeve and then tucked it into her robe.

"You scared me," Jun said.

"You brought a phone with you," Yuki said with amazement.

"What?" Jun said, unconvincingly. "What are you talking about?"

"You have a phone, which means you're from the same time that I am, and you came through a portal to get here," Yuki said. "Why are you even checking your phone? You know there's no Wi-Fi here."

"Yeah, of course I know that," Jun snapped. "But we don't really know how the whole mirror thing works, do we? Something happened to my grandmother before I left. I keep checking my phone in case by some miracle I have a text with an update. My battery's about to die, though."

"Is that the thing you told me about?" Izumi asked Yuki. "The tool that you write letters with?"

"That's the one," Yuki said, adding, "I'm sorry about your grandmother."

Jun shrugged. "Thanks. I should have known. Land of a Merry Cat."

Izumi crossed her arms and frowned. "Well, are you really from Echizen Province?" she asked.

"No," Jun admitted. "I'm from Tokyo. Nobody except Murasaki knows the truth in my group. How come you know about Yuki?"

"Several cycles ago, I walked into Shōnagon's room as a contestant came through the mirror," Izumi said. "The mirror had stretched to the size of a door and suddenly this girl appeared dressed in battle armor and threatened us with a blade. So Shōnagon had to tell me. This contestant promised

112

me that if she won, she would take me and some other girls to the temple and train us to be her ninja spies, which sounded pretty exciting. But she didn't win."

"By the way, just because I'm checking my phone, that doesn't mean I want to go back," Jun said. "I have no intention of going back."

Yuki felt the sting in Jun's words. Yuki had been so busy preparing for the contest that it had been easy to push Hana—and, by extension, her father—from her mind. Being with her mother always reminded her of her father. Probably it was the same for Hana, too. Being apart was better for them both.

Yuki pulled her shoulders back. "Neither do I," she said.

"Well, this has been fun," Jun said. "But I need to go inside before Murasaki notices I'm gone. She's stricter than the teacher who does the dress code check at my school. You're lucky you got Shōnagon."

As Jun sauntered down the path, Yuki couldn't decide whether competing against someone from her own world was going to be better or worse for her tomorrow. But she did agree with one thing that Jun said. She did feel lucky to have Shōnagon.

8

In the First Round
of the Contest

Nervous about the first round, Yuki couldn't sleep. No position on her thin mat felt comfortable. She had sore spots on her hips, her shoulders, and the back of her head. Also, the giggling and gossiping and the opening and closing of doors had gone on into the wee hours. None of it had seemed to bother Izumi, who slept soundly in a cloud of lavender silk. Shōnagon had not returned from the party, as the attendants often stayed in the empress's quarters.

When Yuki could see light trickling through the shutters, she decided to go to the study to look at the *kai-awase* shells and review her scribbled stanzas from yesterday. After gathering up the papers, Yuki folded the pages and tucked them inside her robe. Slipping out of Shōnagon's room, all she could hear was soft, steady breathing and the occasional rustle of silk. She crossed through the covered walkway to the empress's quarters and entered the dim building. The shutters were still closed. That was going to be a problem, Yuki realized, as she made her way to the study. She didn't have a lamp, and she didn't want to get in trouble for opening the shutters by herself. As she pondered what to do, a light bobbed toward her.

"You're up early," Nobu said.

Yuki had looked for him all evening at the party. And now here he was, with his dark hair needing to be brushed out of his eyes and his earnest smile revealing his chipped front tooth. One day she would ask him the story behind that.

"I couldn't sleep," Yuki said. "I thought I'd go to the study. What are you doing here?"

"I offered to open up the aviary," Nobu said. "It gives me an excuse to be in the palace. Do you want to come?"

"Yes, I'd love to see the aviary," Yuki said.

He led her to the back side of the building where they crossed a walkway into another wing. In the dim light, Yuki saw what looked like rows of miniature tents on tables of different heights extending down the long, narrow gallery.

"If you don't mind removing the covers from the cages, I'll take care of the shutters," Nobu said.

Yuki went down the row, taking off the silk covers and waking up birds of all different sizes and colors. Meanwhile, Nobu used a wood box as a step stool to push open and latch the shutters. When he had finished, Nobu took her to each cage and identified the birds. The wood pigeons with iridescent green-purple plumage waddled when they walked. The thrushes with yellow feathers and stark white rings around their eyes could sometimes be seen hanging upside down. The pair of white-and-brown-speckled owls liked to cuddle. In the middle of the aviary, they came to the golden pheasant's empty cage. Broken shards of mirror lay on the floor.

"The mirror must have broken when Okinamaro knocked over the cage," Nobu said.

"Why was there a mirror inside?" Yuki asked.

"The golden pheasant never sang, and the empress was worried that it was sad," Nobu said. "One of the ladies suggested putting a mirror in the cage to make the pheasant think it had a friend. The bird was too smart for that, though."

Nobu found a square cloth in a cupboard and placed the mirror shards in the center. While he wrapped up the pieces, Yuki realized she had an opening to find out if the pheasant had ever spoken to Nobu. "In my country, there are birds called parrots that can talk," she said. "Could the golden pheasant speak?"

"Oh yes," Nobu said with an impish smile. "It said *ken ken*."

Yuki tilted her head and narrowed her eyes at him. "What is *ken ken*?" she asked.

"That's the sound the pheasant makes," Nobu said. "You

know, the rooster says *kokekokkō* and the dog says *wan wan*."

"That's ridiculous," she said. "A barking dog does not sound like *wan wan*."

Nobu grinned. "I didn't invent it," he said. "Why, what does the dog say where you're from?"

"*Woof woof,*" she said.

Nobu burst out laughing. "Perhaps I should send for the imperial doctor to have your ears checked," he said.

"Whoever came up with *wan wan* should have their ears checked," Yuki said. Though if she was the only one who had heard the pheasant speak, maybe she needed to have more than her hearing examined.

"Well, there may be a whole flock of golden pheasants here soon," Nobu said. "Our envoy to China is going to try to bring back more for the empress."

"A group of pheasants is called a bevy, not a flock," Yuki said. The words popped out before she thought about how obnoxious she sounded. "I learned all the special group names for birds," she added quickly. "There's an unkindness of ravens, a bouquet of hummingbirds, and a parliament of owls. My favorite one is a siege of cranes."

"You know a lot about birds for someone from the Land of a Merry Cat," he said. "Do you miss it?"

Nobu was the first person to ask her if she missed home. That kindness made her heart swell. Everyone else seemed to assume that if she was willing to leave her country, then it must not be very interesting.

"There are lots of things I miss," Yuki said. "I miss sleeping in my own bed. I miss wearing my own clothes. I miss hot showers. I miss a lot of foods, most of which you wouldn't know. I miss having waffles with strawberries and maple syrup on Sunday mornings. And these gooey grilled cheese sandwiches that are the only thing worth buying at the school cafeteria. Oh, and Top Ramen, which is this dish of instant noodles in a broth made from a packet that's basically salt and scary-sounding things like bisodium-maltodextrin-glutamate. It's so bad that it's good. Ramen is actually from your country, but it doesn't exist here yet."

Nobu's forehead crinkled. "It doesn't exist here yet," he said. "How does something you eat in your country come from my country and not exist yet?"

Yuki clamped her hand over her mouth. She'd been so careful not to talk about things from her world that wouldn't make sense to the others. But with Nobu, she'd let her guard down. "I shouldn't have said that," she said. "Sorry, I'm going to stop talking about home now."

But Nobu persisted. "Yuki, what did you mean?"

"I can't tell you," Yuki said. "I'm sorry."

"I caught a glimpse of your clothes on your first day, when Okinamaro went into Shōnagon's room," he said. "And it's not only your clothes that are unusual. Every cycle, the contestants seems to know more and more about the world outside the empire, or they refer to things that we do not have here."

118

"I can't speak to the other contestants," Yuki said, "but the Land of a Merry Cat is very different."

Nobu raised his eyebrows. "How did Shōnagon find you?" he asked.

Yuki realized that she and Shōnagon should have worked out a detailed backstory. So far, Shōnagon had managed to brush off any questions with "I have my ways," and the other attendants had not pressed her.

"How did Shōnagon find me," Yuki repeated, her mind spinning. "I believe she wrote a letter to my parents and asked for me to come."

Nobu nodded. "And how does she know your parents?"

"My mother is a distant relative," Yuki said. "A messenger arrived with a letter from Shōnagon, and my parents sent me to court."

Nobu folded his arms and cocked his head to the side. "You're saying Shōnagon asked a royal messenger to locate a ship traveling to a country that we've never heard of before and brought you back," he said.

Yuki felt herself wilt under the pressure. "Not even the regent asked all these questions," she said.

"Whatever your secret is, you can trust me," Nobu said. "I'm not going to report you to the regent. You did save me from decapitation, after all."

"I'm supposed to guilt-trip you with that line, not the other way around," Yuki said.

"You have funny sayings in the Land of a Merry Cat,"

Nobu said. "If your guilt takes you on a journey to the truth, then I am not sorry."

Yuki walked to the next cage and watched the finch-like white birds flutter around inside. Shōnagon had told her not to tell anyone. But could there be any harm in telling Nobu? Yuki thought she could trust him.

"You can't tell anyone what I'm about to tell you," Yuki said. "Only Shōnagon and Izumi know."

"I promise not to tell the oxen," Nobu said. "They are terrible gossips."

"This is going to sound completely made-up," Yuki said. "You're right. I didn't come here by ship. Shōnagon has an enchanted mirror that works as a portal. That's how she finds her contestants. In my world, the portal opens every one hundred years. I'm from the twenty-first century."

"And I traveled to the Dragon King's underwater castle on a turtle's back," Nobu said. "Come on, Yuki. You can tell me."

"That's the truth," Yuki said. "I swear. I came here from another time and place. I guess that makes me a double foreigner."

Nobu sucked in his cheeks and frowned. "I'm not sure what I expected you to say, but it wasn't that." He knotted the corners of the cloth and picked up the bundle of mirror shards.

Yuki shifted her weight nervously from one foot to the other. She hoped the truth wouldn't ruin their friendship.

"As hard as it is to believe, that would explain some things I have seen and heard from other contestants," Nobu said. "Did you choose to come here or was it an accident?"

"I chose to come," she said.

"Why?" he asked. "What was happening in your time?

Yuki realized he must be thinking of war or famine, something epic in scale. Her real reasons for coming suddenly seemed small. "It's a long story," she said. "Family reasons."

Nobu nodded. "You are very brave," he said. "I think if I traveled to your time, I might have regrets. Do you ever wonder if you made a mistake in coming here?"

His question took her breath away. She couldn't have regrets. She wouldn't allow herself to have regrets. "No," she said. "I like it here. And I hope we can still be friends."

"Of course," he said. Though she could tell by the grave look on his face that her secret had deeply affected him. "I should get back to the oxen," he added.

"And I should get back to my studies," she said with a forced smile.

Yuki had a sinking feeling in her stomach as she made her way back to the study. On the day when she should have been completely focused on the contest, all she could think about was whether Nobu would accept her.

While she had been in the aviary, the shutters had been opened in the study. Tearing off tiny squares from her stack of copied poems, Yuki folded origami cranes. She found the repetition soothing.

Hana had taught her how to fold paper cranes for her hundredth day of kindergarten project, where every kid brought in one hundred of something. Yuki loved how the crane body formed a small balloon that had to be inflated through a tiny opening, and how the beak and the tail tapered into a fine point. Once they had one hundred cranes, her mother had stacked them and run a thread through their balloon bodies to connect them. Yuki loved the idea that if you gave someone a string of origami cranes, you were besieging them with good fortune. That's what she needed now. A siege of good fortune.

Yuki sat in front of the mirror on Shōnagon's vanity and painted her face white. She still felt like an actor getting ready for a play, but at least the stark white makeup covered the pimple on her chin. Every time she looked at herself in the mirror, she wondered if the portal would open again and what she would do if it did. The mirror had a much smaller cloudy spot along the edge than the one in Momo's store. If only the mirror would show her what was happening in Santa Dolores. Probably nothing. Probably nobody cared. Her mother had Doug and Julio had Suzie and the kids at Juana Maria Middle School didn't know who she was, except for Zoe, who would be too busy doodling patterns on her arms to notice.

"Here, let me even that out for you," Shōnagon said. She knelt next to the stool and Yuki turned to face her. Shōnagon dabbed at her face with the brush. Yuki wished she had Shōnagon's dainty lips and her bright, knowing eyes. Most of all, she wanted to command a room the way Shōnagon did, with her wit and her words.

Once Yuki's makeup was done, Shōnagon dressed her in a dark red layer, a dark green layer, and then several greens that grew progressively lighter, adjusting each one at the collar and at the sleeves.

"Did Izumi tell you that we saw Jun in the garden last night and found out she came through a mirror, too?" Yuki asked.

"Yes, she did," Shōnagon said breezily. "Well, it's hardly surprising."

"I guess not," Yuki said. "Izumi said Jun had more time to prepare for the contest. I hope I don't let you down."

"You are extremely well prepared," Shōnagon assured her. "My advice is, do not think about what you are doing as creating art. That is much too high a standard. You are like the gardeners who care for the snow mountain. You are moving the snow around and shaping it."

Yuki nodded and decided not to mention that her snow mountain would look like moguls on a ski run.

When they arrived at the empress's quarters, Yuki found Izumi standing with a group of ladies peeking around the blinds and murmuring with concern. Thinking they had spotted the golden pheasant, Yuki went to join them. But she didn't see a bird perched anywhere on the roofline.

"What are you looking at?" Yuki asked.

"The crack in the sky is back," Izumi said. "You can see it above the snow mountain."

Yuki followed her gaze. In the stark blue sky, she made out a faint hairline crack shaped like a lightning bolt. When Shōnagon first told her the story of the crack in the sky, Yuki had thought there had to be a logical explanation. A wisp of cloud, maybe. But the sharp zigzag did not remotely resemble a cloud.

"We're holding the contest just in time," Izumi said.

Yuki's gaze fell on the stage in the courtyard garden where a servant was laying out the *kai-awase* shells in a circle. With the placement of each shell, Yuki's chest grew tighter. Every poem Izumi had drilled into her left her head. Why had Yuki thought the Wonderland Slam meant she was capable of rescuing Shōnagon and fixing the sky?

When the delicate flute music began, the notes swirling like leaves caught in the wind, the three judges proceeded across the courtyard to the stage, each step slow and deliberate. The master of divination sat between the chamberlain and the minister. Nobu was already onstage setting up a timer: a shoebox-size container filled with sand and a pack of incense sticks. Next, the consort and her ladies took their places beneath their canopy. Then Empress Teishi descended the stairs, followed by her retinue. Yuki tried to match Shōnagon's easy, tranquil gait. Once they settled beneath their canopy, the emperor glided to his dais. The flute music waned as the master of divination stepped to the front of the stage.

"Good afternoon, ladies and gentlemen," the master of divination said. "Welcome to the first round of our contest to select the new high priestess of poetry. Today our young poets will compete in *kai-awase*, a challenging game that requires a sharp eye as well as poetic skill."

"How nervous these young ladies must be, playing in front of the entire imperial court," the chamberlain added.

"Yes, how right you are," the master of divination said.

Yuki was so nervous, she thought she might throw up. She looked over her open fan to see if Jun also seemed jittery. Jun was clutching her closed fan in both hands and looked ready to break it in two. Yuki didn't recall being nervous when she competed in the final round of the Wonderland Slam. That had been easier, she realized, because nobody expected good poems from a nine-year-old. All the pressure had been on Ferny Bloom.

"My esteemed master of divination, do you have any predictions for the contest?" the chamberlain asked.

"I wouldn't dare make a prediction about our contestants, except to say this round will be exciting indeed," the master of divination said. "However, I will make one prediction. I predict that our dear chamberlain will not know the answer to this riddle."

Yuki heard the sharp, exasperated flick of courtiers opening their fans. But she was grateful for the delay and was starting to find the patter between the master of divination and the chamberlain endearing.

"Oh, I better put my thinking cap on, then," the chamberlain said.

"No matter how late in the day it is, I never run out of time," the master of divination said. "What am I?"

The chamberlain stroked his beard. "Hmm. There's never enough time in the imperial schedule so I can't imagine what that could be," he said.

"The answer is a sundial," the master of divination said.

"Very clever," the chamberlain said.

Yuki suppressed a smile and looked at Izumi, who rolled her eyes.

"Boooo," a gentleman called out from the crowd. "Did you predict that I was going to say that?" The audience erupted with laughter.

The master of divination waved the courtier's words away. "All right, all right, let's begin our contest," he said. "Ladies, please come up to the stage."

As Yuki stood to follow Shōnagon, Izumi whispered, "Good luck." Nobu gave her an encouraging smile as she stepped onto the platform.

Standing on opposite sides of the shell circle, Shōnagon and Murasaki faced each other and bowed. Following their lead, Yuki turned and bowed to Jun, then knelt next to Shōnagon. A bead of sweat trickled down her chest. She felt like what she was: a scared kid in a costume.

"Our contestants will take turns trying to make a match," the master of divination explained. "Once a match is made, the senior attendant will come up with the first line of the poem and the contestant will finish the poem. Each turn is timed. You must make a match and come up with a poem before the incense stick burns out. If the judges accept the poem, the team earns a point. The team with the most points at the end of the game wins the round. Since Consort Shōshi's team won the last contest, Jun will go first."

A little girl in light pink robes chose a shell from the canister and set it in the center. Nobu lit the stick of incense in the sandbox. Yuki studied the stripes and ridges in case Jun failed to make a match. There was nothing distinctive about this one, which had evenly spaced lines.

"You are at the halfway mark," Nobu said.

Jun picked up the center shell. Then she chose a potential match. Inside her sleeve, the two sides emitted a short screech, which meant they didn't fit together. Once Jun returned the shells to their places, Nobu lit a new stick of incense. Yuki narrowed her choices down to five. But from there she had to guess. She wondered if the set used for the contest was designed to be more difficult than the one she had practiced with. When Nobu announced that her time was halfway up, Yuki grabbed two shells. When she pressed them together, they skidded in her palms.

She and Jun went back and forth, neither getting a match. But Jun had keyed in on the same shells as Yuki. Finally,

Jun smiled with triumph as the two sides clicked into place. She held up the shells to show everyone the interiors, which depicted a sprig of white flowers against a gold background.

"As the last snow melts beneath the sun, I eagerly await the scent of the plum blossom," Murasaki said.

"Let their perfume wrap me in memories, long after their petals have fallen," Jun said.

The judges conferred. "One point for Jun," the master of divination said.

Whoever got the first point had the advantage. Now Yuki felt the pressure to find a match. The little girl set down a new center shell, which had speckles toward the hinge. Yuki thought for certain she'd found its mate. But when she picked them up, the two sides didn't fit.

Jun found two more matches and Yuki started to despair. She glanced at Shōnagon, who remained perfectly composed. She didn't understand how Shōnagon could be so calm. On her next turn, Yuki tried to stop thinking so hard, tried to be serene like Shōnagon. She thought about softening her gaze. She thought about finding a mate and not a match. Yuki chose a shell. A smile broke out across her face as the two sides clicked. The interior paintings showed a winged insect on a tree branch.

"The cries of the cicada echo in the summer night," Shōnagon said.

The cicada. Yuki remembered walking with her mother through a leafy park at dusk in Tokyo and hearing the melancholy chirps for the first time. "If only I could cast off this hollow shell and leave the world of sorrows behind," Yuki said.

She held her breath as the judges conferred. "One point for Yuki," the master of divination said.

After that, Yuki was on a roll, tying Jun at three. But from there, she was constantly playing catch-up. When they tied at nine each and only one match remained, Yuki's heart sank. Jun had the next turn, which meant she would win by default. Picking up a shell in each hand, Jun flipped them over to look at the paintings. Then she dropped the shells as if they had burned her palms. Yuki leaned forward. Based on Jun's reaction, she expected to see something truly strange inside. But the shell interiors showed an ordinary bird with black-and-white-striped tail feathers sitting on a branch with white blossoms.

"Tell me when we shall meet again on the Magpie Bridge," Murasaki said.

Yuki remembered that magpies were part of a story about two lovers only allowed to meet once a year. The magpies had created a bridge in the sky with their feathers for the lovers to cross. Transfixed by the image inside the shell, Jun seemed to be taking rapid shallow breaths. Was Jun having a panic attack because she was on the brink of winning? Murasaki frowned, trying to prod her student with the harshness of her gaze.

"Your time is almost up," Nobu announced.

All Jun had to do was say something about the feathers in the sky. Yuki glanced at Shōnagon, who seemed equally perplexed. Jun's lips moved but no sounds came out.

"Tell me when we shall meet again on the Magpie Bridge," Murasaki repeated.

The warning note in her voice seemed to shake Jun out of her paralysis. "I search the sky for signs of snow-tipped—"

"Time," Nobu said.

Yuki held her breath as the judges bent their heads together.

"No point," the master of divination said.

Jun bowed her head and looked like she might burst into tears. Tight-lipped, Murasaki slid the two shells toward Yuki. Though she felt bad for Jun, Yuki couldn't believe her good fortune.

"In the dead of winter when the magpie calls," Shōnagon said.

"I dream of the feather bridge in the sky and look for you," Yuki said.

"Point to Yuki," the master of divination announced. "Empress Teishi's team wins the first round by a score of ten to nine."

Yuki clasped the shells to her chest. She had won! Shōnagon nudged her and they both stood up and bowed to Murasaki and Jun. Yuki noticed that Jun barely bent at the waist and still looked like she was in shock. Yuki wondered if the magpie had something to do with Jun's grandmother. If there had been a shell with a painting of a carton of milk—of anything that reminded her of the awful last conversation she'd had with her father—Yuki would have been shaken up, too.

"The second round will take place tomorrow during the Hour of the Rooster," the master of divination said. "The competition will be held at the home of the minister."

Once they had all retreated behind the blinds in the empress's quarters, the celebration began.

"My heart is still pounding," Empress Teishi said, exhilarated. "I thought all was lost."

"You did it," Izumi exclaimed, dancing around.

Amid the hubbub, someone handed Yuki a white flower, a globe with its petals closed up tight. Looking around, she spotted the back of Nobu's head as he slipped through a panel door. Her heart did a flip. Nobody had ever given her a flower before.

"That's a peony," Shōnagon told her. "It's a symbol for bravery and good fortune."

For the rest of the evening, Yuki could not stop smiling. Today had been the best day of her life since the Wonderland Slam.

9

In the Second Round
of the Contest

As Yuki stowed her insulated lunch bag inside her locker, the bell rang. How was that possible? She was never tardy. Running down the hall with the rest of the late kids, she dashed into science class, where the other students were already hunched over their desks. Mr. Krash had given them a pop quiz. Krash was short for Krashenninikov. On the first day of school, he'd written his name across the entire dry-erase board and said, "The second *n* is silent." She'd been the only one to laugh. Yuki slid into her seat at the end of the row where the test was waiting for her. The first question read, "Objects in the mirror are closer than they appear. Explain."

Her heart revved with panic. She'd already failed an English assignment. She couldn't fail this quiz, too. Yuki raised her hand.

"Excuse me, Mr. Krash," she said. "I've been absent so I can't take this test."

"Have you ever looked in a mirror?" he asked, folding his hairy arms.

"Well, yes," she said.

"Then you can take the test," he said.

A cow lowed behind her. When Yuki turned in her seat, she found Ava wearing a cow head like the Egyptian goddess Hathor. Ava was looking at a phone with Zoe.

"You think I should be nipped in the butt?" Zoe said. "Oh, Yuki, that's mean."

That had been in a private chat with Julio on LVLup. How could Zoe know about her list?

"Let me see that," Yuki said, trying to grab the phone from Zoe's hand. But Ava mooed a warning at her.

"Oh, didn't you know?" Zoe said. "Julio invited us to join the chat."

Zoe cackled and Ava mooed and Yuki woke up in an unfamiliar room. Next to her, Izumi snored softly. Shōnagon was also asleep, one silk sleeve flung across her forehead. After the party, they had all gone to bed in a room connected to the empress's inner chambers.

The celebration had gone on until dawn amid a flood of congratulatory letters for Yuki and Shōnagon. Some letters came with a sprig of white flowers from the branch that the magpie had been pictured with (viburnum, Shōnagon informed her). Others had a feather attached. Shōnagon also had several admirers come up to the veranda to visit,

133

and Yuki enjoyed listening to their banter. In the wee hours, Yuki and Izumi had played a game similar to backgammon on a beautiful hand-carved set. The playing pieces, in dark and light wood, felt substantial in her hand, not cheap and disposable like the plastic ones she was used to. Yuki suddenly understood Momo's rant about how people here spent every moment trying to make the world more beautiful, while modern-day life was small and limited to a rectangular screen. The palace was not perfect. But she loved that at court everyone aimed for perfection.

Rolling to her side, Yuki touched the peony, which had been a tight ball when Nobu gave it to her but now resembled a ballerina's frilly tutu. She wondered if Shōnagon knew anything about how to press flowers, because Yuki wanted to keep this one forever. Picturing Nobu with his chipped front tooth when he smiled made her heart dance. She couldn't wait to see him again. Maybe this was what a crush felt like.

Unable to go back to sleep, she slipped on her robe and tiptoed out of the room. She headed to the aviary, thinking she might see Nobu. However, it was late enough in the morning that the shutters in the empress's wing had been opened and the servants were bustling about. As Yuki crossed the bridge to the aviary, she heard chirping and felt a twinge of disappointment. If Nobu had taken care of the birds, he'd already come and gone. She visited the aviary anyway, enjoying the birds' chatter and bright eyes.

"Hello," a high whispery voice said.

The golden pheasant. Yuki turned around in a circle but didn't see the bird.

"Up here," it said.

She looked up and found the pheasant perched on top of its empty cage. "You're in the aviary," she said. "I thought you didn't like your cage."

"Nobody will ever think to look for me here," the pheasant said, puffing out its wings.

"Good point," she said, taking a bowl from the gilded cage. Then she took a bowl from another cage and poured half the birdseed into it. She sat on the floor and set the bowl down for the pheasant, who landed next to her and pecked at the seeds. It looked at her with its warm wide eyes.

"You are my friend," the bird said.

Yuki resisted the temptation to scoop the pheasant into her arms and give it a hug, since birds probably didn't like being held. She wished she could take the pheasant home with her. Having a talking bird was the coolest thing ever. "You're my friend, too," she said.

"I have only had one other friend in the palace," the pheasant said. "But my friend was scrolled."

"The last time I saw you, you told me to beware of the scrolling," Yuki said. "What is the scrolling?"

The pheasant pecked at the seeds and then cocked its head thoughtfully. "The scrolling is how you lose yourself," the bird said.

Yuki frowned. The pheasant's explanation was even more

confusing. "When you say scrolling, do you mean a scroll like a rolled-up piece of paper?" she asked.

"It is rolled like a piece of paper and kept like a piece of paper," the pheasant said. "But it is not paper."

"Then what is it?" Yuki asked.

"I do not know the exact word," the pheasant said. "A double."

Before Yuki could press for more details, Izumi hurried through the aviary entrance.

"There you are!" Izumi exclaimed. "The master of divination sent over instructions for the second round. Shōnagon has ordered a carriage. We're going on an excursion."

When Yuki looked around for the pheasant, the bird was gone.

As they waited for the carriage, Shōnagon explained that the second round was going to have a summer theme and she wanted Yuki to experience the season firsthand. Yuki was excited to leave the palace compound and see what the rest of the capital looked like. From the veranda, she stood with Izumi and Shōnagon and watched a group of servants push a two-wheeled carriage toward the stairs. Once the back door of the carriage was level with the steps, Yuki climbed inside. Izumi and Shōnagon crawled in behind her and then arranged their robes so that their hems dangled out from beneath the blind covering the door.

"Why are you doing that?" Yuki asked.

"To show off our color combinations," Izumi said.

"Otherwise, the ladies and gentlemen who pass by won't know how fine we look."

Through a crack in the front curtain, Yuki watched the men grab the carriage shafts and pull. The carriage groaned and lurched forward. The attendants brought the carriage to a gate where Nobu and a man with an ox on a lead line waited. Yuki hoped that meant Nobu was coming along. Maybe she'd get the chance to talk to him. While Nobu helped hitch the ox, another carriage pulled up beside them.

Shōnagon tutted with displeasure. "Look at that," she said. "The young ladies in Murasaki's group are wearing those ridiculous newfangled robes that are made with an extra-wide sleeve on one side just for the purpose of hanging out of the carriage. The extra-wide sleeve is very unpleasing to the eye. Don't they realize that once they leave the carriage, this makes them look lopsided? I must add this to my list of distasteful things."

Yuki studied the silks hanging out the back of Murasaki's carriage. She wasn't sure how Shōnagon could tell that their sleeves were extra wide.

"Some girls at my school wear these puff-sleeved shirts that make their shoulders look like wings," Yuki said. "Those don't look right, either."

"The extra-wide sleeve is by far worse," Shōnagon declared. "At least your puffy shirt is symmetrical."

Yuki loved that Shōnagon was debating which was the greater fashion disaster with her. It reminded her of the lists that she and her father used to make, ranking the Beatles albums or the Harry Potter books or movies based on books, and then arguing about which deserved the top spot. *The White Album* versus *Magical Mystery Tour. Goblet of Fire* versus *Prisoner of Azkaban.* They had both agreed on *The Princess Bride.*

Once the ox was hitched, the handler and Nobu walked by the ox's head while the other men flanked the carriage. As they exited the inner palace compound, Shōnagon called out to the driver to take them past the Great Hall of State. Lifting the window blind, Yuki saw a massive hall with red pillars and green roof tiles. The driver then took them through a large courtyard dotted with pine trees. Izumi pointed out the various administrative buildings that lined the courtyard. The bureau for books and drawings. The folk music office. The sewing office.

After the ox plodded through another gate, Shōnagon said they were now on the streets of the capital. A pothole sent Yuki backward into Izumi's lap. Another dip sent a comb flying out of Shōnagon's hair. Riding through the capital was like Mr. Toad's Wild Ride in slow motion. Yuki grabbed the window frame to keep from falling over and pulled back the blind. They passed courtiers on horseback and more ox-drawn carriages with silks flapping out the back.

Soon high walls lined the road on either side. Izumi pointed out the gate to the minister's villa where they would gather that evening for the contest. When the mansions gave way to green countryside, the ox moved into a trot. The driver, Nobu, and the attendants broke into a jog, their footfalls landing in unison. The smell of sage filled the carriage.

When the carriage stopped in a clearing near a river, Shōnagon handed Yuki a wide-brimmed white hat with a veil to put on her head, which she said was proper attire for ladies outdoors. Nobu unhitched the ox, and then the attendants helped Shōnagon, Izumi, and Yuki out through the front of the carriage onto a mat that had been laid on the ground to keep their robes from getting dirty.

"The judges will likely choose the cuckoo for your poem," Izumi said as they strolled up to the orange trees. "But they might also go with the orange blossom."

"The last time the minister hosted, we had to place our poems in little boats that floated along a stream to the judges," Shōnagon recalled, "so you must be prepared for anything."

While the attendants set up portable tables and writing boxes beneath the orange trees, Yuki turned to look at the river. The opposite side appeared to be blanketed in an eerily dense fog. She lifted her veil to make sure. It was worse than the evening fog in Santa Dolores. Once, she had been driving back from the library with Doug and the fog had been so thick that he'd had to roll down the window in order to see the double yellow line on the road. Yuki had clutched the plastic door handle for dear life, as if that would protect her if they drove into a ditch or another car crashed into them. Even though Doug always drove the speed limit and used his blinker and was probably the safest driver she could get caught in the fog with, she had hated the feeling that they could be blindsided at any moment and there was nothing she could do.

"That is the Tedium," Shōnagon said, following her gaze. "Just thinking about being inside that fog gives me the most unpleasant feeling. Like seeing the back of a piece of embroidery, or a row of sniffly children."

Yuki thought everyone had been exaggerating about the Tedium, the way people who lived on the Westside of Los Angeles expressed horror about going to the San Fernando Valley. Now that she saw it, the Tedium did seem to mark the edge of a void. She couldn't imagine anyone living inside it.

"How do the people who are banished there survive?" Yuki asked.

Izumi snorted. "They don't survive for long," she said. "They are eaten for dinner by the demons and ogres."

A look of contemplation crossed Shōnagon's face. "Once I went on a pilgrimage to a temple where I met a priest who claimed to visit the Tedium regularly," she said. "Of course, I was horrified. But then he told me something quite unexpected. He said that the exiles have created their own villages and have completely adapted to the lack of sunlight. They have remarkable hearing, and because they are aware of his footsteps, even from a great distance, the exiles are always waiting for him in their village square. I accused the priest of telling fairy tales. But I must admit there is something romantic about it."

"Very romantic," Izumi said. "Until an ogre turns you into a midday snack."

The other carriage had parked downstream from them. Jun and two ladies-in-waiting were in fact wearing robes with a wider sleeve on one side, which made them look like sailboats listing in a harbor. Murasaki had on traditional-style robes. As Yuki watched them, she realized that in a meadow past the orange grove, snow was falling.

"Is that real snow?" she asked, not believing her eyes.

"Of course," Izumi said. "I'm so glad we aren't doing winter poems today. It isn't nearly as pleasant to sit over there. My favorite place is autumn, though. That section has deer and bush clover. I like to feed the deer rice crackers."

Yuki had only seen snow fall once, when she was little and they went to spend Christmas with her father's family in Chicago. Mesmerized, she walked to the edge of the meadow and watched the fluffy snow land on the pine trees. She caught a snowflake on her palm and watched it melt on impact. Izumi came up to her and tugged on her sleeve.

"We should get to work," Izumi said. "You need to focus on summer, not winter."

Yuki sat down at the portable table next to her mat and began to make ink, grinding the black ink stick against the stone. Meanwhile, Shōnagon broke off a twig from an orange tree and set it next to Yuki's writing box. The glossy green leaves and five-petaled white blossoms seemed exactly like the ones on the orange tree in their backyard in Santa Dolores, though the fruit looked closer in size to a tangerine.

From somewhere in the trees, a bird chirped.

"That is the cuckoo," Shōnagon informed her. "There is nothing else like it."

Yuki listened to the birdcall. She thought she had a good ear, since she and her father used to play their own personal game of *Name That Tune*, listening to the classic rock station in the car and seeing who could name the next song the fastest. But the truth was, to her ear the cuckoo sounded like any other bird.

Izumi cracked open a poetry anthology. "The cuckoo is a messenger between our world and the spirit world," she explained. "Remember that. And the cuckoo is often associated with orange blossoms, which evoke fond memories of the past. Remember that, too."

Yuki hoped she wouldn't have to remember too many associations, or she would get them all jumbled up in her head. Izumi read some cuckoo poems to her. Yuki jotted notes and then tried to come up with her own cuckoo poem. She wanted to work in the orange blossoms, too, and take care of two topics with one poem.

"What do you think of this?" Yuki asked, offering her poem to Izumi. But Izumi wasn't paying attention. She was studying Shōnagon and Murasaki, who stood near each other clipping sprigs from the same orange tree.

Izumi frowned. "Can you tell if they're speaking to each other?" she asked.

"Not from here," Yuki said. "Why?"

"I came up behind them once and they were definitely speaking to each other," Izumi said. "As soon as they noticed me, Shōnagon shooed me away. They tell people they don't like each other. Yet they always wind up near each other during this outing."

"Maybe they're talking about writerly things," Yuki said. "What makes you think something suspicious is going on?"

Izumi shook her head. "I don't know," she said. "It's just this feeling I get when I see them talking to each other. I can't really explain it."

Since the trees were short and squat, Yuki thought they could get close to Shōnagon and Murasaki without them noticing. "We might be able to hear what they're saying from that tree over there," Yuki said, pointing to the nearest one. "If they see us, you start telling me everything I need to know about the orange blossom."

Yuki and Izumi moved until they could see Murasaki and Shōnagon in profile through a gap in the branches of the tree. Murasaki examined an orange that she held in her palm while Shōnagon clipped sprigs and laid them in a basket.

"Sometimes I think I would like to lose three in a row and be done with this," Murasaki said. "I am tired."

Yuki exchanged a surprised look with Izumi. This did not sound like the same Murasaki who had coolly jabbed at Shōnagon in front of the regent.

"Don't be ridiculous," Shōnagon said in a subdued tone. "You will never finish your tale of Genji if you are decapitated.

Besides, the regent would simply replace you with another writer and nothing would change."

"We are trapped by our own ambitions," Murasaki said. "Still, I have bad dreams."

Just then, the two haughty ladies in extra-wide sleeves approached, whispering to each other and giggling. Murasaki and Shōnagon moved farther apart. Yuki and Izumi returned to their portable writing desks.

"I don't understand," Izumi said as she ground her ink stick against the stone. "Winning the contest is an incredible honor. How can Murasaki be tired of it?"

Yuki wondered if Murasaki didn't like the stress of the contest. Maybe Murasaki had dreams like Yuki did about failing pop quizzes. But when Shōnagon said nothing would change anyway, what did that mean? Did that have something to do with the pheasant's warning? None of it made sense.

"Sometimes when I complain about school, my mom says she would love to trade places with me and be a student again," Yuki said. "She says there are too many things to worry about once you're an adult. Why doesn't Murasaki have a helper to train her contestants?"

"The consort's ladies don't like her very much," Izumi said. "They say she keeps to herself. She probably wouldn't trust anyone else to help her."

Yuki read over her poem again. But she couldn't focus on the words. She was too restless. Standing up to stretch, she spotted Nobu at the river's edge with the ox. He was talking to Jun. Yuki could only hear the cadence of their voices. Jun might have been asking Nobu for ox-handling tips, yet resentment welled up in Yuki, as it had when Julio had told her about passing notes with Suzie in computer class. She was convinced that the Suzies of the world would always overshadow her.

"Don't let him distract you," Izumi said crossly. "At least put him to good use and practice by writing him a poem."

Yuki knelt before the portable desk with her brush hovering over a clean sheet of paper. "What should I say?" she asked.

"How about something about the flower he gave you," Izumi said. "Like, 'Petals tossed upon the wayward wind. So fleeting is the white peony.'"

"I don't know," Yuki said. "Is that judging him? Is he the white peony?"

"No, the white peony is love," Izumi said. "It's supposed to be poetic."

"It *is* poetic," Yuki assured her. "I'm worried it's too much." If she had learned anything from the LVLup disaster, it was to be more careful about her words.

"Forget it," Yuki said, closing the writing box. "I'm going to talk to him instead."

As Yuki marched toward the river, the ox driver called out to Nobu. Before Yuki could get his attention, Nobu turned around and led the ox away. That left her standing by Jun, who picked up a rock, flicked her wrist, and skipped the stone across the water. The rock skimmed the surface four, five, six times and then disappeared into the river.

"Wow, you're good at that," Yuki said. "My dad tried to teach me, but I could never get the stone to skip more than twice."

Jun found another smooth, flat rock. This one skipped all the way to the other side and disappeared into the Tedium. "I spent a lot of boring summers in the country," Jun said. "There was nothing else to do."

"What happened yesterday?" Yuki asked. "You looked like you saw a ghost."

Jun's face clouded over and she kept her eyes on the ground, hunting for skipping stones. "My grandmother collects antiques," Jun said. "She has a wall hanging with the same bird painting. It freaked me out, seeing that."

Yuki had the distinct feeling that there was more to it. But Jun kept hunting for rocks and didn't say anything more. "That would freak me out, too," Yuki said. "Is your grandmother the one who had Murasaki's mirror?"

Jun nodded. "The mirror was her favorite piece," she said. "My grandmother must have told me the story about Murasaki inviting someone to her side of the mirror about a million times. I've been hearing that story since I was, like, two."

"Was coming here something you wanted to do for a long time, then?" Yuki asked.

Jun's laugh had a bitter tinge. "I would have gone anywhere

the mirror wanted to take me," she said. "I needed to get out of Tokyo fast."

"Why? What happened?" Yuki was intrigued. Jun had that surly attitude that teachers hated. Yuki could see her breaking all kinds of rules.

"Like I would tell you," Jun said, crouching to examine more rocks.

"Yeah, well, I was having a situation, too," Yuki said with all the bravado she could muster. "Then I looked in the mirror and there was Shōnagon. I had to make a snap decision."

"Let me guess," Jun said. "You got less than a perfect grade on a test."

"Oh, yeah, sure, because that would be the end of the world," Yuki said with sarcasm, now that the red 48 was firmly in the past. "It's family stuff. My mom married this guy."

That piqued Jun's interest. "Does he have a criminal record or something?" she asked.

"He should," Yuki said. If she were in charge, she'd sentence Doug to diagramming every bad joke he'd ever told.

Jun walked farther downstream, and Yuki took the hint. It was probably better not to be too friendly. They were competing, after all. Yuki went back to the orange grove and worked on poems. All too soon, the time came to leave for the minister's villa. As soon as Murasaki's carriage rolled out of sight, Shōnagon told the ox driver to take a detour.

"We'll be late," Izumi warned.

Shōnagon waved her hand. "Nobody cares what time you arrive as long as you make an impression," she said.

The carriage stopped alongside a row of tall hedges with clusters of white blossoms that stretched skyward. White lilac, Izumi told her, which was also associated with summer and the cuckoo. Shōnagon asked the runners to cut branches and decorate the carriage. The men laid lengths of white lilac on the roof and wedged them in the windows while Nobu added a sprig to the ox's halter. With so many branches crisscrossing inside, Shōnagon, Izumi, and Yuki could barely fit.

"What is this spectacle?" the minister exclaimed when they rolled through his gate. "Your carriage looks ready to fly to the heavens. I can hardly believe there are people inside."

As Yuki climbed out, she caught a glimpse of Murasaki watching them with disapproval. She guessed Murasaki and Shōnagon wouldn't agree on whether it was good form to make a splashy entrance. Empress Teishi and the rest of her ladies were waiting for them inside the villa.

"Your arrival caused quite a stir," the empress said, looking pleased.

In a room created out of folding screens, Yuki, Izumi, and Shōnagon changed into new robes and touched up their makeup. Then they gathered with Empress Teishi and the other attendants. Yuki peeked around the blinds at the courtyard and the large lake on the other side. A meandering stream cut across the courtyard at a diagonal. Where the stream met the lake, a stage had been set up. The minister had decided that the spectators would board dragon boats and watch the contest from the water. Once all the boats had been launched, music from a flute and a drum drifted over the water from an island in the middle of the lake.

From the top of the main staircase, the consort and her attendants descended to the courtyard. Except for Murasaki, they all wore the robes with extra-wide sleeves. Next Empress Teishi, her bearing softer but more regal, crossed the courtyard with her ladies-in-waiting. Then the emperor and his aides filed down to the courtyard. Once all the royals had boarded their boats, the music shifted to something more dramatic. Shōnagon and Murasaki walked side by side down the stairs. Yuki and Jun followed them. Instead of getting into a boat, the four of them stepped onto the low stage where the three judges awaited them. The master of divination stood to address the audience.

"Today marks the second round of our contest to name the next high priestess of poetry," he said. "Many thanks to the minister for opening his home to us. What a delightful scene this is with all of you on the lake. Now, this is not the only surprise that our dear minister has in store for us. He always enjoys adding something special and unexpected. Let me give you a hint: I only work when I'm in the water. But I can't swim. What am I?"

"Could it be seaweed?" the chamberlain asked.

"Seaweed doesn't do any work," the minister pointed out. "It merely floats about."

149

"No, it's not seaweed," the master of divination said. "Any more guesses?"

"A ship or a boat," Yuki said under her breath.

"Nobody knows the answer?" the master of divination said. "All right, then. Page boys, come on up."

Two young boys stepped up onto the stage holding toy boats.

"The answer is a boat!" the master of divination exclaimed. "Today's game will add the element of a race. Lady Shikibu and Lady Shōnagon will take their places upstream while Jun and Yuki will be stationed at the midway point. When the topic is announced, Lady Shikibu and Lady Shōnagon will write their poems and place them inside these boats and send them floating down the stream to Jun and Yuki. The contestants will read the poems and add their responses. The first boat to reach the judges will gain an extra point. The poems will then be read aloud and the judges will cast their votes."

Yuki was suddenly gripped by anxiety. What if she reached for the boat and fell into the stream? What if she dropped her poem into the water? She didn't like this at all.

"Ladies, you may take your places," the master of divination said.

The page boys led them off the stage. Murasaki and Jun crossed a footbridge to the other side of the stream. At the midway point, two portable tables had been set, one on either side.

"Let your words flow like this stream," Shōnagon said in parting.

Yuki sat on the mat in front of her table and ground the ink stick against the stone. Time seemed to speed up and slow down. Shōnagon and Murasaki took forever to walk to their tables at the top of the stream, yet they also arrived too soon. In the lull, cicadas rattled. Frogs croaked. Waves lapped against the dragon boats. Yuki's mouth went dry.

"Hey, Yuki," Jun called out. "You're going down this time."

"That's right," Yuki retorted. "Downstream. All the way for the win."

She somehow managed to sound bold even as doubts continued to clamor in her head. To shut down her thoughts, Yuki swirled some ink on a spare piece of paper, forming a large, nervous blot.

"Your topic is the cuckoo bird," the master of divination announced. "Poets, you may begin."

Yuki moved closer to the stream's edge so that she'd be ready to catch the boat. Since they'd already prepared for the cuckoo as a theme, Shōnagon and Murasaki wrote furiously. They took their finished poems and folded them into skinny strips with a knot in the center while the page boys held the boats in the water. After Shōnagon and Murasaki set their poems inside, the page boys released the boats. Yuki willed Shōnagon's to pull ahead as the two boats disappeared briefly beneath a footbridge. But when the boats emerged, they were still coasting along side by side. As they started to drift toward the center, Yuki felt a flutter of panic. Her worst fear was coming true. If she reached too far to grab the boat, she'd fall into the stream. Taking a fresh ink brush from the writing box, she stretched her arm over the water and used the handle as an extension to stop the prow and guide the boat toward her. Jun copied her, and they both managed to angle their boats toward the edge without losing the poems.

Yuki unknotted the paper and smoothed out the page. *At last! The white lilacs are in bloom. How long must I wait to hear the cuckoo's song?*

Okay, it was a love poem. A poem about waiting for someone to show up. Yuki didn't know anything about romantic love. But she knew how it felt to wait. She saw Jun start to write and the pressure built in her brain, pushing against her skull. Yuki moved words around like the square pieces in a slide puzzle. *Cuckoo. Lilac. At last!* But the words stayed jumbled up. When Jun lifted her brush from the paper, Yuki thought all was lost. Instead of folding the page, Jun chewed nervously on the end of the brush handle. Yuki still had a chance. She wrote:

O cuckoo, bird of summer, where have you gone?
At last! I hear you in the lilacs. I am not alone.

Yuki dropped her brush and folded the paper into a strip, nearly tearing it in half as she tied the knot in the middle. Tucking both poems inside the boat, she pushed the vessel downstream. Her boat was about a foot ahead of Jun's. *Go, go, go,* she thought. As her boat approached the footbridge,

Yuki stood to get a better view. Suddenly a rock plunked in the water and knocked her boat over on its side. The two knotted poems floated on the surface, the water staining the paper until the ink bled.

10

*Distressing and
Surprising Things*

One of Yuki's earliest memories was a birthday party at an indoor bouncy-house place where there had been ice cream cake and disco balls and music with loud, thumping bass. She had rushed into the scrum of four-year-olds to snag the last purple balloon, which she had planned to tie to a Lego Friends character and pretend the tiny doll was Dorothy flying away from Oz. But on the way home, Hana had decided to get the car washed. When Yuki opened the door to get out of the car, the string had slipped off her wrist and the purple balloon floated into the sky. She watched with heartbreak and horror as it went higher and higher until it became a tiny dot.

That's how she felt now as the waterlogged poems sank into the stream.

When Yuki's capsized boat drifted out to the other side of the footbridge, the crowd gasped. Meanwhile, Jun's boat cruised ahead. Only one person could have hit her boat with a rock. Yuki glared at Jun.

"You cheated," Yuki said.

Jun ignored her, pumping her fist inside her sleeve as the minister bent over and picked up her boat at the finish line. Yuki said it louder: "You cheated. You sank my boat with a rock."

She was about to call out to the judges when Shōnagon appeared at her side.

"Stay calm," Shōnagon said. "Complaining will only hurt your cause."

"She was skipping rocks at the river earlier," Yuki said in an indignant whisper. "I know she did it."

"If the footbridge blocked the judges' view, there's nothing to be done," Shōnagon said.

On the other side of the stream, Murasaki joined Jun, and they started walking toward the stage. This was the Pokémon card incident all over again. Yuki had witnessed Jun doing a bad thing. Yet by pointing it out, somehow Yuki was to blame.

"What was your poem?" Shōnagon asked.

Yuki repeated what she had written.

"Excellent," Shōnagon said with a nod of approval. "You should be proud."

Tears filled Yuki's eyes. She was happy and sad. Happy

that Shōnagon liked her poem. Sad that she had let Shōnagon down.

"Hold your head high," Shōnagon whispered as they approached the stage. "We'll win tomorrow. There shouldn't be any races or games in the final round. Only poetry."

Her confidence was a small consolation to Yuki, who barely registered the reading of the poems to the audience. After the judges conferred, the master of divination announced the obvious, that Consort Shōshi's team had won. As the servants set up a post-contest feast, Shōnagon arranged for Yuki and Izumi to immediately take the carriage back to the palace.

"You have to beat her tomorrow," Izumi fumed as they bumped along the road. "We can't have a high priestess with poor character. What if Amaterasu realizes the high priestess assigned to her is a cheater? She'll be offended. Then the crack in the sky will only become worse!"

Yuki peered out the window. The jagged white line seemed more pronounced amid the stars in the night sky. But that might have been her imagination. "Why didn't Shōnagon say anything? I don't understand," she said.

"Because Jun is sneaky," Izumi said. "From the dragon boats, all we saw was that your boat had tipped over. If the judges heard you accuse Jun of cheating, they'd consider you to be ill-mannered. They might hold it against you at tomorrow's contest."

"So it's all right to cheat, but not all right to complain about the cheater," Yuki groused.

Because everyone else was still at the party, the living quarters around the garden were dark and quiet. From the veranda by Shōnagon's room, Yuki watched fireflies winking in the bushes.

"Do you want to practice some more?" Izumi asked, joining her.

Yuki shook her head. "I need a break tonight."

"Well, we should do something besides sit here and think about how awful Jun is," Izumi said.

"I have an idea," piped up a voice in the dark. Nobu jogged up the steps.

"I can't imagine what that is, since all a stable boy knows is how to pick up ox poop," Izumi said.

"I'm surprised, Izumi, that such an uncultured thought entered your head," Nobu said with a wry smile.

"There's a big difference between knowing an ox poops and having to clean it up," Izumi said.

"Everybody poops," Yuki said. That had been the title of Julio's favorite book when they were five. "Even you, Izumi," she added.

"Ew," Izumi said, covering her ears.

Nobu cracked up. Yuki loved being part of the banter, and especially loved feeling like she was the edgy one.

"*Everybody Poops* is the name of a book in my world, by a writer from your country," Yuki said.

"There's a book about poop? Then I shall never go to the Land of a Merry Cat," Izumi wailed.

They all laughed, even Izumi. And the fireflies winked as

if they, too, were amused.

"What's your idea?" Yuki asked Nobu.

"There's a place I like to go that always cheers me up," he said. "But we would have to sneak in."

"That's a terrible idea, then," Izumi said sharply.

"You don't have to come," Nobu said. "I asked Yuki."

Truth or dare. That's what this moment felt like, minus the truth, which is what Yuki picked whenever she got roped into that awful game. She'd watched in horror once as Julio licked a slug and Troy ding-dong-ditched old Mrs. Cratchett who lived on the corner. But truth was hardly better, since Maddie had once asked who Yuki would rather kiss, Julio or Troy. When Yuki had said "neither," Maddie, Julio, and Troy gleefully shouted "liar" and made kissing noises at her. But she couldn't tell the truth, because if she admitted that she'd rather kiss Julio than Troy, that might have made things weird between her and Julio. Not that she wanted to kiss him. He was like a brother. But she definitely did not want to kiss Troy, who always had peanut butter breath and an odd hiccupy laugh.

"Sure, why not?" Yuki said in her new, more daring persona.

Yuki rose to follow Nobu. They went around to the back side of the attendants' quarters and down the stairs into a narrow courtyard.

"If you get caught, you'll be banished to the Tedium," Izumi called out from the veranda. "Or worse! Nobody's going to save you from decapitation this time, Nobu."

158

"You sound like a brown-eared bulbul," Nobu said.

Yuki giggled. She had no idea what a bulbul was, but it sounded funny. Izumi gave an exaggerated sigh and hurried after them. After passing the wing containing the aviary, they walked toward a cluster of buildings where the palace officials worked. Nobu stopped in front of a building with double doors. Both doors had circles painted in the center. The left door had a black circle against a white backdrop, while the right door had a white circle against a black back-drop. Both circles had small red dots peppered across them, just like the tunics that the master of divination and the chamberlain wore.

"That's creepy," Yuki said. "The doors look like a pair of eyes watching us."

"Those aren't eyeballs," Izumi informed her. "They're star charts. The red dots are the constellations."

"Those are the offices of the master of divination and the chamberlain," Nobu said. "Besides being in charge of the calendar, the chamberlain is the keeper of all royal doc-uments."

Nobu took them around to the left side of the building, where a short breezeway connected to a separate wing. He knelt on the ground next to the attached building and removed a wood panel, revealing a crawl space beneath.

"What are you doing?" Izumi demanded.

"Going into the archive," Nobu said. "I promise, it's a sight beyond words."

"Have you been possessed by a fox spirit, Nobu?" Izumi

159

wondered. "What would ever make you think to crawl beneath a building?"

"Do you remember when Empress Teishi's cat disappeared?" Nobu asked.

"She seems to always be losing her pets," Yuki noted.

"The empress used to have a cat named Lady Rokujo," Izumi said. "But the cat is not at the palace anymore. Lady Rokujo was sent to live with the empress's parents."

"Well, I'm the one who found her," Nobu said. "I heard meowing and discovered a creature had dug a hole beneath this panel. I popped the panel out and found Lady Rokujo in here with five kittens."

Yuki laughed. "Does anyone ever confuse Lady Rokujo with an actual lady?"

"The empress's cat is a lady of the fourth rank," Izumi said gravely. "To live in the palace, pets must at least have risen to the fifth rank."

"Pets have ranks?" Yuki asked.

"Oh yes, we have a ministry for that," Izumi said. "On the day that the rankings are announced each year, the courtiers gather with their cats and dogs. You can tell by how high they hold their tails if they've received a promotion."

"I would like to see that," Yuki said wistfully.

Izumi and Yuki tucked their hems into their waistbands to keep their robes from getting dirty. Bending over, they followed Nobu into the crawl space. Nobu lit a lantern that he kept inside, revealing a series of wood posts supporting the floor of the archive. Then he leaned the panel back in place so that anyone passing by would not notice it had been moved.

In the middle of the crawl space, Nobu stepped onto a stool, removed four planks overhead, and clambered into the archive. Yuki climbed on the stool and popped her head through the hole, scoping out the interior like a prairie dog. Nobu's secret entry was between two rows of shelving lit by a floating paper lantern.

He reached out to pull her up. Yuki felt awkward grabbing his hand. But she also didn't trust that she had the strength and coordination to climb through the hole on her own. She wiped her sweaty palms on her robe first. Then she held her breath as he grasped her hand and pulled her through. Once she was inside, Yuki stood in the middle of the row and looked up. Spirals in every hue of the crayon box filled each shelf. They looked like snail shells glowing in the soft lamplight. With a gasp, she realized the spirals were rolled-up letters. Paper scrolls.

"They're so beautiful," she said.

"Don't touch the scrolls," Nobu warned her as he turned to help Izumi. "Or the floating lantern will wake up and scream."

"What do you mean?" Yuki asked.

But Nobu didn't answer because he was struggling to help Izumi, who had gone limp like a sack of potatoes. Yuki wandered to the end of the row. They had come up between the fourth and fifth rows, and there were eight in all. Somehow the archive seemed much larger on the inside than it had from the outside. Yuki felt like she had stepped into a sacred space, a church devoted to paper. She wandered toward the entrance, pausing to study the constellations that decorated the double doors. To the left of the doors hung a painting of a crow chasing a rabbit.

When Yuki went back to join Nobu and Izumi, they were staring up at the lantern.

"I've never seen an enchanted lantern before," Izumi said. "I've only heard about them in ghost stories. Those top two rips must be the eyes and the lower one the mouth."

"How did you wake one up?" Yuki asked Nobu.

"One scroll was sticking out and I pushed it back in," Nobu said. "Big mistake. The lantern screamed and tried to catch me with its tongue. I almost didn't make it back to the crawl space in time."

Nobu lay down on the floor with his hands behind his head, gazing at the scrolls. Yuki copied him. She couldn't decide what she loved more, the snow mountain or the archive. A metallic glint midway up the shelving caught her eye. One scroll had a rainbow-tinted coppery hue around the edge like a snail's trail after the rain.

That prompted Yuki to tell Izumi and Nobu about how she and Julio used to follow the shimmery snail trails and move the snails from her mother's garden to the compost pile. That led to another story about the snail poem she wrote for the Wonderland Slam, the words forming a curlicue. Then she told them about her father starting the poetry slam and teaching philosophy classes on *Alice's Adventures in Wonderland* and *Through the Looking-Glass*. And that led her to tell them about how she and Julio watched *The Wizard of Oz* every year before Halloween, which meant she also had to explain what a movie was and what Halloween was. And then she told them about how her mother and Julio's mother scoured the internet and the garment district every year to make her costume and Julio's by hand. She wasn't used to being the kid who entertained everyone with stories, but Nobu and Izumi hung on her every word.

"Having a family sounds nice," Nobu said.

Yuki froze. "You have a family, don't you?" she asked.

"I believe I do," Nobu said. "But it's hard to remember anything about my life before coming to court."

"It's very fuzzy, isn't it?" Izumi said. "My clearest memories are the contests. I can't picture my sisters or my mother anymore."

"I get the feeling time works differently here," Yuki said. "Is it—is it lonely, being at court all the time?"

"I hadn't thought about it until I met you," Nobu said. "I suppose it is."

"We're always around other people and we're always busy," Izumi said. "But it does feel lonely sometimes."

Yuki had thought she couldn't get away from her life fast enough. But talking about her childhood made her realize how much good there had been, too. Nobu and Izumi didn't really get to be kids. They had to act like mini adults at court. While Shōnagon looked out for them, she was more like a cool aunt than a mother.

Izumi leaned back on her elbows. "I have to admit it," she said. "This wasn't a horrible idea."

"Told you," Nobu said, pleased.

"You still smell like an ox," Izumi said.

"And you still sound like a brown-eared bulbul," he said. "Besides, I didn't invite you. Remember? You invited yourself."

"I came for Yuki," she said.

"So did I," he said.

Yuki was glad that the three of them had their eyes fixed on the scrolls and not on each other because she couldn't stop smiling. Julio had been her best friend by default. They'd grown up together. This was the first time she'd chosen her friends, and they had chosen her back.

11

In the Third Round
of the Contest

"Yuki, come quickly," Izumi called out. "Shōnagon is about to read the contest instructions."

Yuki had escaped to the veranda and was studying the crack in the sky. All morning long, courtiers had been stopping by the empress's quarters to commiserate with Shōnagon and express their dismay that Yuki's boat had been knocked over by a frog. That was the story Jun had told everyone. Yuki was so enraged that Jun had turned Kermit into a scapegoat that she decided to watch the gardeners cover the snow mountain in order to calm down. That's how she discovered the crack had deepened and widened and now arced over the entire courtyard. She hadn't believed the sky could break into jagged pieces and fall until now.

Yuki followed Izumi into the reception room, where all the attendants and little girls had gathered. The empress motioned for Yuki to come sit next to her. Then Shōnagon read the letter out loud.

"'For the third and final round, Empress Teishi and her team will dress in teal, and Consort Shōshi and her team will wear red,'" Shōnagon said. "'Each team will also create a decorative display to present at the contest. In this round, the contestants will not receive any help from Lady Shōnagon and Lady Shikibu. Topics will be announced and the first contestant to finish her poem will raise her paddle. Her poem will be read aloud by an assigned reader, and then the other contestant will have a chance to respond. The judges will vote, raising a teal paddle or a red paddle to show whose poem they thought was best.'"

"Can they throw the dragon?" Izumi asked.

"Yes, they can," Shōnagon said. "I'm just getting to that. 'After the response has been made but before the judges have awarded their points, the poet who went first can raise her paddle and throw the dragon.' Yuki, that means you have a chance to make a rebuttal. But you must be certain the judges will rule in your favor. Throwing the dragon is all or nothing. You either win the whole contest or you lose."

Yuki nodded, but she was barely taking it in. Like when Doug took her and Hana to a Dodgers game and tried to show her how to use the chart in the program to track each play. There had been too many symbols to remember, too many rules to follow.

The ladies-in-waiting discussed ideas for the display and decided to go with snow, in Yuki's honor. Then everyone

166

got to work. The attendants created an alpine scene on a low stand about the size of a small coffee table and sent the little girls out to the garden to find white flower petals and pine twigs. In another room, servants perfumed robes for the contest, draping them over bamboo stands with incense burners inside. Soon the empress's quarters smelled like a Christmas tree lot.

Yuki and Izumi went to the study to prepare. Izumi opened the container of *kai-awase* shells so that Yuki could practice making poems on a wide range of subjects.

"This round is much more difficult," Izumi said. "Instead of building on each other, you're trying to make it hard for the other person to respond to your poem. The worst thing you can do is end your poem with a question. If Jun responds with something clever, the judges' points will all go to her. With the response, you'll always want to make a joke at Jun's expense if you can. Nothing vulgar, though. It needs to be witty."

Yuki felt the stirrings of a headache. There was always so much to remember. Izumi took a shell out of the canister and flipped it over to reveal a pheasant. After the disastrous second round, Yuki had forgotten all about the pheasant's warning.

"Izumi, do you know what scrolling is?" Yuki asked.

"I know what a scroll is," Izumi said. "But I've never heard of scrolling."

"It's something I overheard," Yuki said. "I think it has to do with the contest."

"There is an official ceremony when the winner becomes high priestess," Izumi said. "But I've never been allowed to see it."

The scrolling is how you lose yourself, the golden pheasant had said. Maybe the scrolling only affected the loser, then. "If I lose, what happens once the contest is over?" Yuki asked.

"Don't say that," Izumi said, placing her hands over her ears as if blocking out the words would keep it from happening. "You're not going to lose."

"I'm not planning on it," Yuki said. "I just want to be prepared."

"The loser has a few minutes to say goodbye," Izumi said. "Then they leave with Murasaki or Shōnagon. Some guards will also be there to escort you. That's been the rule ever since the ninja threatened the judges with a sword after she lost."

Yuki was tempted to go look for the pheasant and try to find out more about the scrolling. But Izumi would be upset with her if she took time away from studying. Besides, the scrolling couldn't be anything bad. Shōnagon wouldn't let anything terrible happen to her. The pheasant had to be mistaken.

"Yuki, I need you to make me a promise," Izumi said.

"Of course," Yuki said. "Anything."

"Will you write to me every day from the temple?" Izumi asked.

Yuki smiled. Finally, someone who loved letter writing as much as she did. It had been so easy to make friends at the palace. She would be sad not to see Nobu and Izumi every day.

"I will," Yuki said, "as long as you promise to write me back."

Izumi smiled as she blinked back tears. "We better get to work," she said.

When they had finished practicing, Yuki retreated to Shōnagon's room. She needed some time alone. The other ladies coming over to wish her luck and the endless chitchat had worn her out. Sitting in front of Shōnagon's vanity, Yuki wondered if this would be the last time she would gaze into the mirror. She touched the cloudy spot. The mirror's surface was cool and hard beneath her fingertips. What was her mother doing right now? What was Julio doing? Were they thinking of her? Yuki suddenly felt an intense ache in her chest. She might not see her mother again, at least not for a long time. Should she write a note to Hana in case she won? She could ask Jun to take the letter through the mirror and then mail it on the other side. If a phone could pass through the mirror, then so could a letter. Yuki could offer to take a letter for Jun's grandmother in exchange—as long as Hana didn't ground her for the rest of her life as a punishment, which was a distinct possibility.

Yuki had a gut feeling that Shōnagon wouldn't approve of her making a deal with Jun, which meant she had only a small window to send a note. She dashed off a letter to Jun proposing the exchange and suggesting that they trade letters beneath the wisteria at the Hour of the Monkey. Flagging a page boy in the corridor, Yuki gave him instructions to deliver the letter directly to Jun and then leave without telling anyone who the note was from.

Once the page boy left, she wrote a letter for her mother.

Dear Mom,
If you're getting this letter in the mail, that means I won
a big poetry contest that's kind of like the Wonderland
Slam, and I will be staying here for a while. Please don't
worry about me. I'm having the adventure of a lifetime!
Love,
Yuki

On the back of the letter, she copied down her address in Santa Dolores.

Much to Yuki's relief, neither Izumi nor Shōnagon had come to the room by the time the guards announced the Hour of the Monkey. She wouldn't have to lie about where she was going. Slipping down the stairs, she hurried through the garden to the arbor. But Jun wasn't there. Yuki paced back and forth nervously, ducking behind a tree when a gardener passed by. Jun had mentioned that Murasaki was strict. Maybe Jun couldn't get away. Or maybe Jun was ignoring her. Disappointed, she returned to Shōnagon's room, where she found Izumi sitting on the stool at the vanity and painting her face white. Yuki braced for a lecture on how she shouldn't be wandering off this close to the contest. But Izumi was somber.

"You should start getting ready" was all she said.

"Do you want me to comb out your hair first?" Yuki asked. Izumi was going to serve as Yuki's reader onstage.

"Thanks," Izumi said.

Yuki dipped the comb in rice water and started at the crown of Izumi's head, brushing through her silky black tresses all the way to the floor. Helping each other with their makeup and hair felt normal now, even if Yuki still felt like she was getting ready for Halloween. When Yuki finished, they traded places. Izumi had just finished combing out Yuki's hair when Shōnagon burst in with a maid carrying the teal robes for the contest.

"How splendid you both look," Shōnagon said. "Nothing can compare to the excitement of the final round of the contest."

Despite her animated words, Shōnagon seemed subdued. And who could blame her? If Yuki failed, Shōnagon would have her memories drained. Yuki couldn't imagine the imperial court without Shōnagon.

"Shōnagon, how does decapitation work? Does it hurt?" Yuki asked.

"I believe it's a spell of some kind, and completely painless," Shōnagon said, sitting down to do her own makeup. "I shall be just fine. Don't you worry."

When they finished dressing, the three of them stood in

a circle and faced each other. Yuki had never played a team sport and had never worn a uniform. Seeing them in matching outfits, a wave of something—maybe gratitude, maybe love—washed over her.

Izumi's chin quivered. "Shōnagon, if the judges don't favor us, will we have a chance to say goodbye to you?"

"I believe I will be taken away immediately," Shōnagon said. "But it is better that way. Izumi, if this is the outcome, then you must capture the moment as the opening scene in your own pillow book, showing how I met my fate with dignity and grace! Now what should my final words be in the event of a loss? One must be prepared for any occasion. Shall I speak of the immortal depths of the Asuka River? Or of the fragile blossoms that will last a thousand years? So much depends on the image."

Shōnagon knelt at her writing desk and wrote with great concentration. Yuki thought maybe her calm and her focus came from knowing she would always be remembered for her words, no matter what happened tonight.

When a servant knocked with a message, Yuki's heart rate spiked. What if the message was from Jun, and Yuki had to explain why they were corresponding?

"From an admirer," the servant said as she handed a fan to Yuki.

The fan had a snowy mountain painted on the front. A message had been written on the back slats: *May the sun shine on the snowcapped mountain. This humble ox is forever in your debt.*

Yuki wished she had more time with Nobu. She wanted to hit pause and live in this moment forever. But time kept moving forward and the fan had already become part of the past. Yuki thought it would be cool to have a mirror like Shōnagon's that let you visit only your favorite memories and relive them whenever you wanted.

When they lined up for the procession in front of the Purple Sanctum, the vastness of the courtyard made Yuki feel very small. The only greenery was a lone cherry tree on one side of the stairs and a mandarin tree on the other. Yuki kept trying to catch Jun's eye. But Jun kept her back turned, which was infuriating. After what had happened in the last round, Yuki should have been the one snubbing Jun. But she was sucking it up because this would be her only chance to let Hana know that she was okay. How could Jun pass up the opportunity to send a note to her grandmother? That only made sense if Jun had done something unforgivable.

The three judges led the procession up the broad staircase into the Purple Sanctum. A group of girls dressed in red followed them, carrying the consort's team display, a lotus pond created out of blue feathers, bamboo leaves, and purple flower buds. Murasaki, Jun, and another female attendant who was serving as Jun's reader trailed them.

"The lotus is an allusion to Jun's name," Izumi said. "'Jun' means purity, and the lotus is a symbol of purity."

"She needs a new name, then, because she plays dirty," Yuki said.

The empress's girls picked up the snow mountain display

and carried it up the stairs. Shōnagon, Izumi, and Yuki fell into line behind them. Inside the hall, Yuki saw the emperor and empress seated on an elevated platform at the far end. They each had their own throne inside a curtained gazebo. Emperor Ichijō slouched in his seat and waved a fan while Empress Teishi perched on her smaller throne with the air of a celebrity on the red carpet. Courtiers lined the perimeter between the royal platform and the stage.

The two groups of girls carrying the displays paraded past the emperor and the empress. Then they set the displays on either side of the stage. The girls in teal knelt in front of the snow mountain, and the girls in red knelt in front of the lotus pond. Shōnagon, Izumi, and Yuki took their places next to the girls in teal while Murasaki and Jun joined the girls in red. Yuki saw Nobu setting up the timekeeper on the stage and touched the fan, which she had tucked inside her sleeve.

Once everyone had taken their places, the master of divination rose and addressed the audience from the stage.

"Welcome, everyone, to the final round of the contest to name the high priestess of poetry," he said. "Look at these wonderful displays from our two teams, a snowy mountain and a lotus pond. How clever. Girls, I want to share with you a most curious thing that happened on my way to the Purple Sanctum. I heard one wall call out to another wall. Can you guess what the first wall said?"

"Oh my, I haven't the foggiest idea," the chamberlain said.

"'I'll meet you at the corner,'" the master of divination said.

The adults in the audience groaned, but the girls who had carried the displays giggled.

"Speaking of walls, see if you can figure out this one," the master of divination said. "I make my own home and it is very small. Yet it is highly valued by emperors and empresses. What am I?"

A girl from Consort Shōshi's team timidly asked, "Is it a silkworm?"

"Yes!" the master of divination said. "The answer is a silkworm. I think this young lady is now the front-runner for our riddle contest at the moon-viewing party. Nicely done."

The girl's face lit up and the girls around her exclaimed with excitement. Yuki thought it was sweet that the master of divination was trying to include the kids. She felt a twinge of guilt for being so hard on Doug.

"After two rounds of competition between Yuki and Jun, the score is tied," the master of divination said. "Tonight, we devote ourselves to pure poetry. Our two contestants will compete without assistance from Lady Shōnagon and Lady Shikibu. When the topic is given, the timer will start and the first contestant to come up with a poem will raise their paddle. Once the poem is read aloud, the second contestant will have the same amount of time to respond. We judges will hold up either a red flag or a teal flag to award our points. However, before we raise our flags, the first contestant may throw the dragon and write a final response. But ladies, you must use this power wisely, as throwing the dragon ends the contest. May the best poet win."

Yuki stepped onto the stage and bowed to Jun, who still wouldn't meet her eyes. *Unbelievable*, Yuki thought as she knelt at her table, where she found a writing box, a stack of paper, and a teal paddle. But she couldn't let Jun get to her. She needed to clear her mind and keep her focus on the contest. Opening the box, Yuki chose a brush and dipped it in the ink, which had already been made. She thought everyone in the Purple Sanctum must be able to hear her heart thumping.

The page boy sitting next to Nobu had a basket filled with paper slips, and he chose one. "The first topic is the willow tree," he said.

Yuki had grown up associating the willow with weeping. But she remembered in this world, the willow had to do with spring, with rebirth. She wrote swiftly: *Dew sparkles in the willows at dawn, like jeweled threads woven into memories of spring*. Then she grabbed her paddle. But Jun raised hers a split second faster.

Jun's reader took the paper from her and recited the poem: "'The willow threads dangle and twist in the spring breeze. But who is to blame for the tangling in my heart?'"

Jun had ended her poem with a question, and Yuki pounced. Before the first ashes from the incense stick had landed in the sandbox, Yuki handed Izumi her response. She

176

saw the corner of Izumi's mouth crick upward with approval. "'The turbulent breezes have left the poor willow in disarray,'" Izumi read. "'I have no use for your knotted threads.'"

Shouts of glee came from the audience. At home, Hana always complained if Yuki was sassy. Here they openly cheered for it. All three judges raised a teal flag. Yuki wanted to leap to her feet and do a happy dance. She'd struck first and hard. But she knew she needed to keep her game face on and not react.

The page boy pulled another slip of paper from the basket. "The kerria rose," he said.

Yuki knew this one, too. The kerria rose was a summery yellow flower that grew in the mountains. This time, Yuki raised her paddle first. The judges gave her two points and Jun one.

They wrote about fireflies and warblers and the autumn moon. They wrote about crickets and herbs and bamboo. The master of divination had not said at the outset how many poems they would have to write. But Yuki could see that only two slips remained.

"The arrowroot," the page boy announced.

Yuki was stumped. She had no idea what the arrowroot looked like or what it symbolized. As she dipped her brush in the ink, the various images inside the *kai-awase* shells flashed through her mind. She felt certain the arrowroot had not come up in her practice sessions, and she could not fake her way through a poem. Glancing over at Jun, Yuki hoped to see her similarly stuck. But no. Jun finished writing, raised her paddle, and handed her poem to her reader.

"'Through the wild storm, the vines of the arrowroot hold fast. Your foolish, flighty winds are no match.'"

Yuki heard the audience exclaim with approval. She needed a sharp comeback. But her brain froze. She was completely gridlocked, like the 101 freeway at rush hour. As the last of the incense stick burned, she wrote: *The fickle storm may change direction as it pleases. But at least it moves freely, unlike the stodgy arrowroot.*

The master of divination and the chamberlain each raised a red flag while the minister held up a teal flag. Yuki and Jun were now tied. The entire contest would come down to this last poem.

"Your final topic is the mandarin duck," the page boy said.

Yuki wrote furiously and raised her paddle. Izumi took the poem from her and recited, "'Through long summer days and cold winter nights, I wait for you by the reed-filled pond. Like the mandarin duck, my love knows no season.'"

Yuki saw the judges nod and she smiled. She thought her poem was airtight. Nobu lit the incense stick. Chewing on the end of her brush, Jun stared at her blank paper. Nothing would give Yuki more satisfaction than Jun not being able to come up with a response at all. When three-quarters of the incense had burned, Jun wrote hurriedly and handed off her poem.

"'When I gaze upon the steadfast mandarin ducks in the

reed-filled pond, I think of my lord, and tears of joy drench my sleeves.'"

A gasp ran through the crowd. Yuki pumped her fist inside her sleeve. Jun's poem about the emperor was smarmy and insincere. She was obviously trying to win through flattery. But then why did Murasaki look so smug? Why were Nobu's eyes welling with concern? Why had Izumi's face fallen? Yuki saw the master of divination, the minister, and the chamberlain reaching for their paddles.

She realized the judges liked smarminess and insincerity and flattery. Jun was going to win. Yuki snatched up her paddle and waved it high in the air.

"I throw the dragon," she said.

12

Throwing the Dragon, Part 1

In Yuki's one and only Wonderland Slam, Ferny Bloom had won the final. But Yuki had been the star. After she read her poem on how a raven was like a writing desk, the professors and students had jumped out of their seats and cheered. Her father lifted her in his arms, spun her around, and exclaimed, "That was fabulous, Monster!" Though she remembered that Ferny Bloom's poem had been elegant and smart and witty, she had been so dazed and dazzled by her own turn onstage that later she could not recall a single word he had said. For coming in first, Ferny Bloom won a thimble and a cash prize. As the runner-up, Yuki received a box that had been labeled "comfits" on the outside but actually contained candy from See's. Ferny jokingly offered to trade the candy for the thimble. Then, over fizzy drinks and an assortment of snacks, teachers and students all came over to congratulate her and say that she would be a great writer one day. And now here she was, on the verge of greatness—as long as she came up with one more poem.

Yuki set a clean sheet of paper on her writing table and touched the fan from Nobu. Then she closed her eyes and pictured the snow mountain.

"The dragon has been thrown," the master of divination said. "Page boy, please start the timer."

Nobu lit the incense stick. Shōnagon had not advised Yuki to praise the emperor given the opportunity, and Yuki could not write something so fawning. She could only write what was in her heart, whether it was popular or not. The words came to her at once, in a rush. She dipped her brush in the ink and hurried to catch up with them. Then she handed Izumi her poem.

"'You speak of mandarin ducks and dampening your sleeves in reed-choked waters. What a pity that the pond should be so shallow.'"

There was a pause—a caesura, as Yuki had learned in English class—while her words landed. Then the crowd roared with delight and the judges threw up their teal paddles. Unanimous. She had won. Yuki was the next high priestess of poetry.

She wanted to run and hug Shōnagon. She wanted to jump up and down with Izumi and Nobu. But she sensed that any celebration would have to wait until they left the Purple Sanctum. Yuki turned to look at Shōnagon, who appeared more relieved than excited. It had been a close call. Empress Teishi, however, exuded the triumphant assurance of a movie star who already knew her name was in the Oscar envelope.

"Yuki wins the third and final round of our competition," the master of divination said. "Congratulations to Empress Teishi, Shōnagon, and the teal team on their victory. Tonight, during the Hour of the Rat, Yuki will be initiated as our new high priestess, and we will offer our most gifted poet to the great goddess Amaterasu."

Shōnagon joined Yuki on the stage. For winning, aides to the emperor presented Yuki and Shōnagon with silk robes and cedar boxes with more trinkets inside. As Yuki accepted the gifts, she saw a flash out of the corner of her eye. Then she heard the girls sitting closest to the stage scream. Shock registered on the faces of the judges. Yuki turned to see a wild-eyed Jun brandishing a dagger at the two guards who had appeared at the side of the platform.

"I'm not going back," Jun shouted. "You can't make me."

Jumping down from the stage, Jun darted behind an ornamental screen that served as a backdrop for the consort and her entourage. The guards chased after her. More guards appeared to whisk the emperor and the empress off to safety as the event came to an awkward end.

"Oh my, there hasn't been this much excitement since the ninja lost," Shōnagon said as they crossed the breezeway back to the empress's quarters.

"And to think Jun came so close to winning!" Lady Hyōbu said with a shudder. "That would have been disastrous!"

"Enough about Jun," Empress Teishi said. "You did it, Yuki! You were brilliant!"

"And to win in such dramatic fashion," Shōnagon said approvingly. "This will go down in the annals as a victory for the ages."

"I can't believe I threw the dragon," Yuki said in a daze. "I'd forgotten all about it until I realized Jun was about to win."

"You were perfect," Izumi said, bouncing up and down on her toes. "And now my best friend in the whole world is high priestess. Please, Shōnagon, can I visit her at the temple?"

Yuki was so thrilled to be called a best friend that she almost missed the flicker of concern pass through Shōnagon's eyes. Yuki hated it when grown-ups thought they were protecting kids by not telling them the truth. But then the flicker was gone and Shōnagon spoke with her usual aplomb.

"Yes, Izumi, I will see if I can get permission for you to visit," she promised.

To celebrate, Empress Teishi ordered dessert. Servants brought in large bowls filled with mounds of shaved ice and syrup to pour on top. A slew of congratulatory notes arrived, from Murasaki, the consort, the emperor, the regent, the judges, and courtiers that Yuki didn't know. Many letters had mandarin duck feathers attached. A group of ladies brought out their instruments and performed a buoyant song. The little girls who had carried the snow mountain display taught Yuki how to dance. Soon they were all swooping their arms and spinning around on a sugar high. Winning felt like her birthday and Christmas and the Wonderland Slam all in one.

"High priestess," a page boy called out, "I have a message for you."

The title, *her* title, sounded strange to her ears. When Yuki tried to stop mid-whirl, her robes twisted around her feet and she collapsed to the floor with Izumi in a fit of giggles. The celebration would have been perfect, except Nobu wasn't there.

As soon as she saw the white peony attached to the letter in the page boy's hand, she realized Nobu was there, in spirit. In the letter, he wrote: *No matter how far you travel, this mandarin duck awaits your return.* She marveled at his confidence and that he wasn't afraid to express his feelings.

"Tell him that I'll write back as soon as we get to the temple," Yuki said to the page boy. Now she owed Nobu two responses, one for the message on the fan and one for this. Somehow, in this world, she was the one making others wait.

"They let Nobu help with the contest, so why can't he stay for the party?" Yuki said, pouting to Izumi.

"He'll probably get to accompany you on the carriage ride to the temple and I'll have to stay here," Izumi said, also pouting.

When Yuki heard the guards outside announce the Hour of the Rat, the room went quiet and all the ladies turned to look at her. This was it. She would be initiated and then she would be traveling to the temple, joining the former high priestesses. What if she didn't like them and they didn't like her? What if she hated her life at the temple as much as she hated Santa Dolores? It hadn't occurred to her that she would be starting over.

"I hope the other high priestesses are nice," Yuki said, sad that she would not be Shōnagon's student anymore, disappointed that she would not go on any more secret excursions with Izumi and Nobu.

"They must be," Izumi said. "Shōnagon has never complained when she's gone to visit."

"Really?" Yuki said, perking up. "What does she say about them?"

"Shōnagon doesn't say anything, actually," Izumi said with a frown. "She's very secretive about her visits."

"Well, now she'll have to let you in on the secret," Yuki said. "I wonder if the guards found Jun."

"I'm sure they did," Izumi said. "They wouldn't stop looking until they caught her. Can you imagine someone like that being our high priestess?"

"She was desperate," Yuki said, understanding the impulse even if she would never make a scene like that.

One by one, each attendant came up to Yuki to congratulate her and wish her well, until only the empress remained.

"This is for your pillow book," Empress Teishi proclaimed, presenting her with a stack of creamy white paper that had heft to it.

"Thank you, Empress Teishi," Yuki said, touched by the gesture. "I'd rather have this paper than all the jewels in the empire."

A maid took the paper from Yuki to pack with the rest of

her things. Then Shōnagon nodded. It was time to go. Yuki turned to Izumi and grasped her hand.

"I'll write to you tomorrow," Izumi said.

"Not if I write you first," Yuki said.

Shōnagon was silent as they left the empress's quarters. When they reached the veranda, she paused by the rail and gazed at the garden. Yuki couldn't tell if Shōnagon was looking at the snow mountain in the moonlight or at the fractured night sky. She did not seem as jubilant about the victory as Yuki had expected.

"You look sad," Yuki said.

Shōnagon gave her a rueful smile. "The end of the contest is always bittersweet," she said. "Your company has been delightful, and I shall miss having you as my protégé."

"But you're going to come visit me, right?" Yuki asked. She flashed to that gut-wrenching moment standing on the lawn between her house and Julio's as the moving truck pulled away. Why did this feel like a goodbye?

"Yes, and what a fine time we will have," Shōnagon said. "But first, you must be initiated as the high priestess. The ceremony will take place in Destiny Hall where the imperial regalia is stored. The regalia includes Amaterasu's mirror. Do you know the story?"

"I do," Yuki said. "My father read it to me. Amaterasu had a fight with her brother and was so upset that she hid in a cave, making the world go dark. The gods begged and pleaded with her. When she wouldn't come out, they hung a mirror in a tree outside the cave and threw a big party.

When Amaterasu asked what was happening, they said they had found a new and even more beautiful goddess. Amaterasu peeked outside and saw her own reflection. Then the gods were able to grab her and pull her outside, and the sun was restored."

"Yes, that's right. Because of that, the mirror contains her essence," Shōnagon said. "To gaze into her mirror is an incredible privilege."

They zigzagged through covered walkways to the east side of the compound. Two guards were stationed in front of a small gate at Destiny Hall. After greeting the guards, Shōnagon led Yuki up a flight of stairs covered by extended eaves. At the top of the stairs, the golden pheasant perched on the veranda railing. Yuki flinched at the sight of the bird.

"Beware of the scrolling, my friend," the pheasant called out.

She'd been so excited to win that she'd forgotten all about the pheasant. Behind Yuki, the guards pounded up the staircase, shouting, "There it is!" As they pushed past Shōnagon, the pheasant flapped its wings, landed on the ground, and darted around the side of the building.

"What on earth do you think you're doing?" Shōnagon snapped at the guards. "How dare you shove me aside. I should report you to the regent."

"Sorry, my lady," one of the guards said miserably. "The empress is offering a reward for her golden pheasant."

"Stomping around is hardly the way to catch a bird," Shōnagon said. "A basket worm has more brains in its head than you."

"We're sorry, Lady Shōnagon," the other guard said, as they sheepishly descended the stairs.

"Hateful indeed," Shōnagon muttered as she approached the double doors, each of which had a large gold seal in the center with the royal chrysanthemum imprint.

Yuki was relieved that the pheasant had escaped the guards. Clearly, nobody except for her had heard the bird speak. "Shōnagon, does the ceremony involve a scrolling?" she asked.

"A scrolling," Shōnagon repeated as she opened the door to the hall. "What does that mean?"

"I don't know," Yuki said. "I was hoping you would know."

Destiny Hall was lit by dozens of candles. In the middle of the room, a round mirror the size of a large pizza had been set on a low table. A gold folding screen separated the table from the back of the room where a large panel door had a monster painted on it, a red ogre that looked even more menacing in the flickering candlelight. The master of divination and the chamberlain suddenly stepped out from behind the screen. Yuki had assumed the ceremony would be attended by more people and would be less spooky and solemn. She wished her mother could be here, in the background, like at a school event. The pheasant risking its freedom to give her one last warning had made her uneasy.

"Congratulations on your victory, Yuki," the master of divination said. "We are honored to have you as our new high priestess of poetry. As you can see from the state of the sky, there's no time to waste. In the initiation ceremony, you will offer your poetic powers to the great goddess Amaterasu. Now please take your place in front of the mirror."

As Yuki knelt before the table, she heard ghostly sighs, a melancholy sound that she decided had to be wind in the eaves. Shōnagon knelt to her left, far enough away that Yuki felt the distance between them. In the candlelight, she made out the inscription around the mirror's edge: *Serve this mirror as my soul, just as you would serve me.*

The chamberlain set a silver tray on the table. The tray held what looked like a slightly flattened wood tube, about a foot long with gold caps at either end.

"Please unsheathe the knife," the master of divination said.

Yuki picked up the tube, which she realized was a knife handle and a cover. She pulled her hands apart, and the blade slid out.

"Now gaze into the mirror," he said.

Yuki did as she was told and looked at her reflection. She had the fleeting thought that she should be able to see the transformation from her sorry Santa Dolores self into this more daring, more accomplished person she had become at court. But she still looked like her old self, only with her hair flattened and parted down the middle and white powder on her face.

"Starting at the top, run the blade inside the edge of the mirror," the master of divination instructed. "Then you will peel off your reflection, roll it up, and say, 'I place my art in the service of Amaterasu.'"

Yuki touched the mirror's surface with her hand. It felt solid and cold beneath her fingers, like a mirror should. But when she placed the blade at the top of the mirror and pressed, a bronze bead welled around the tip. *Beware of the scrolling*, the pheasant had said. Was this the scrolling? She pulled the knife back.

"Why do I have to give Amaterasu my reflection?" she asked. "I thought I just had to write poems in her honor every day."

"By giving Amaterasu your mirror reflection, you are vowing to place your inspiration for writing, your reflections, in her service," Shōnagon said.

"Will I still be able to see myself in a mirror afterward?" Yuki asked.

Shōnagon paused and her eyes flitted over to the master of divination. "I don't know," she said. "I have never asked."

The possibility of not seeing anything at all in a mirror freaked Yuki out. If you couldn't see yourself, did you still exist? Besides, looking at your reflection came in handy, to make sure you didn't have a cowlick in your hair or food stuck in your teeth. Winning the contest had been the greatest thing that she'd ever done. But now she felt torn.

"You have proven yourself worthy and will be the greatest poet in the land," the master of divination proclaimed. "This is the small sacrifice that Amaterasu asks of you."

Yuki had that feeling she used to get at the doctor's office when she was little and didn't want to get a shot. That's how the master of divination was looking at her, like he was trying to convince her that the needle wouldn't hurt. She thought about how Shōnagon calmly went into each round of the contest with her memory at stake and how she took the time to write what could have been her last words. The master of divination was right. Being high priestess and writing poetry—being remembered for her poetry—was the most important thing Yuki could do.

She pressed the blade into the mirror again. As she ran the knife clockwise around the edge, bronze gel oozed from the cut. The glimmering reminded her of something. But what? The mirror suddenly misted over, from the edges to the center. Then the cloud dissipated, and images flashed past. Riding in the car with her father and singing "I Am the Walrus." Playing cards with Julio inside a blanket fort. Folding a hundred origami cranes with her mother. Wearing an itchy black dress at the funeral. Wearing an equally itchy lavender dress at the wedding. Memories that she'd forgotten and that she'd never forget passed through the mirror. Maybe that was what this sacrifice was all about. Saying goodbye to your past.

When she'd cut almost all the way around, Yuki glanced over at Shōnagon, who gave her a tight smile. Something didn't seem right. The outer edge of her reflection began to curl inward. When she reached the top, Yuki set down the knife and touched the edge with her finger. Even though the metallic gel looked wet, it was dry to the touch. *Beware of the scrolling.* Wait, when Shōnagon had said that decapitation was a spell that took away a person's memories, was this how it was done? But that didn't make sense. Yuki wouldn't be able to write poems for Amaterasu and keep the sky from falling if that was the case. And really, what could a pheasant who spent most of its time in a cage know? This was the last step that had to be taken if Yuki wanted to be high priestess. As she started to peel off her reflection, the mirror showed an image that couldn't have been a memory at all.

Julio, his eyes full of mourning, holding up a note that read: COMƎ HOMƎ.

13

*Even More Distressing
and Surprising Things*

Jolted by the sight of Julio, Yuki nearly fell over backward. As she reached out to him, her fingers pressed against the mirror's surface, which felt surprisingly soft and gelatinous, like it might let her in if she kept pushing. But then his image clouded over and the mirror hardened again. Yuki didn't understand what was happening. She only knew that everything felt wrong, like she had stumbled off the scrambler at the county fair after eating too much cotton candy.

"I'm sorry, I can't do this," she said.

Yuki fled the candlelit hall and ran along a path without considering where she was going. Where could she go? Not to the empress's quarters. Not to Shōnagon's room. There was only one safe place. The ox stable. She remembered that when they went to hear the cuckoo birds, the carriage had been hitched at one of the eastern gates not far from the Purple Sanctum. Scanning the rooflines, she located the Purple Sanctum and realized she'd been running in the wrong direction. Yuki climbed a flight of stairs and hurried along a covered walkway, holding her fan up to her face in case she passed a servant or a courtier. In the distance, she heard the head guard shouting out names for the nightly roll call and the guards twanging their bows in response. Thankfully this part of the compound was quiet since most of the buildings were used for storing things, like the treasury and the armory. When she could see the side of the Purple Sanctum, Yuki went downstairs into a small courtyard. Standing in the shadows to get her bearings, she thought she heard snorting. As she crossed the courtyard, she caught the distinct whiff of livestock. She kept walking around the building, following the snorts and the smell until she found the barn entrance.

"Nobu?" she called softly. "Nobu? Are you here?"

The oxen rustled in their stalls. A light bobbed as Nobu stepped into the aisle and held up a lantern.

"Yuki?" His voice sounded drowsy. "What's wrong?"

"I didn't have anywhere else to go," she said. "Shōnagon took me to the ceremony. But it was spooky and weird and I was supposed to cut off my reflection and even though the pheasant warned me not to, I started to do it anyway. But really, how are you supposed to make sure you don't have food stuck in your teeth if you no longer have a reflection? Then I saw my friend Julio in the mirror and I ran out."

Nobu took in the torrent of words blankly. When she finished, she stood there taking ragged breaths and trying not to cry.

"Is that all?" Nobu said.

Then he laughed a laugh that lit up his whole face, and she laughed with him. An ox draped in a red silk blanket nuzzled her shoulder. Something about the animal's attempt to comfort her forced up a sob. Tears started spilling down her face. Nobu led her to an empty stall and folded up an ox blanket for her to sit on.

"Tell me again," he said. "But more slowly this time."

She told him all about the ceremony, feeling better just being with Nobu and the oxen.

"Does this mean you no longer wish to be the high priestess?" he asked.

"I don't know," she said. "When I saw Julio holding a message to come home, I couldn't go through with it. Shōnagon wasn't happy or excited at the ceremony. She seemed troubled."

"Maybe it's because she'll miss you," Nobu said.

"I don't think that was it," Yuki said. "I feel like she's not telling me something."

"We could go look for the golden pheasant," Nobu suggested.

His brow had furrowed when Yuki told him about the pheasant calling out a warning. But he had accepted this seemingly impossible account without question, and for that Yuki was grateful.

"I never find the pheasant," Yuki said. "It always finds me."

"That could be because you don't speak to it in its language." Nobu stood up and raised the shutter. "*Ken ken! Ken ken!*" he called out the window, making the sound of a pheasant.

"You're ridiculous," she said. But she couldn't help giggling.

"At least I made you laugh," he said, leaning one shoulder against the wall and grinning. "I asked the ox drivers which of them had been assigned to take you to the temple because I wanted to come along. They laughed and said after every contest this is the big mystery. None of them has ever taken the high priestess to the temple. They joked that the master of divination must have a secret carriage."

"That's strange," Yuki said.

"You called?" The high whispery voice came from the window.

Yuki and Nobu looked up and found the pheasant perched on the sill.

"You came," Yuki said with amazement.

The pheasant fluttered to the floor and brushed the side of its head against her arm. "I will always come if you call," the bird said. "Even though *ken ken* is not how a pheasant sounds to another pheasant, I understand that is how humans hear us."

"It's talking," Nobu said, dumbfounded.

"You can hear it?" Yuki said, excited to not be the only

one. Nobu nodded, transfixed.

"Pheasant, I didn't go through with the ceremony," Yuki said. "I didn't cut my reflection."

The pheasant bobbed its head. "Reflection. That is the word I was seeking," the bird said. "Not double."

"So cutting off your reflection from the mirror is the scrolling," Yuki said. "How did you find out about this?"

"My other friend was the first high priestess," the pheasant said. "I went inside to watch. Nobody knew I was there. After the scrolling, she lost herself."

Yuki exchanged a confused look with Nobu. "What does that mean, pheasant?" Nobu asked.

"The priestess did not know Shōnagon," the pheasant said. "She did not know anyone. She did not know her own name."

"She lost her sense of self," Yuki said. "Her memory was gone. The scrolling is decapitation." She shivered. If she'd gone through with the scrolling, she would have been like Alice in the wood where things have no names—only forever.

Nobu slumped against the wall. "Oh, that is terrible," he said. "What happened to the priestesses after the scrolling?"

"They do not leave the palace after they are scrolled," the pheasant said. "I hear them behind the demon door."

"There's a door in Destiny Hall with the painting of a monster on it," Yuki said. "Is that where the priestesses are?"

"Yes, that is the demon door," the pheasant said.

"Shōnagon and Murasaki know this," Yuki said. "Shōnagon was going to let this happen to me."

She was so stunned, she could hardly breathe. Why were the grown-ups in her life always letting her down? Shōnagon had made Yuki believe that she was special, that she was talented, that she was fulfilling her destiny. But it had all been a lie.

"I can't believe this," Nobu said angrily. "How can they be so cruel?"

Yuki wanted to hide in the stable and never leave. But the truth was, the guards would find her eventually.

"What should I do?" Yuki asked. "I can't stay here. How do I go home?"

"I could try to take Shōnagon's mirror from her room and bring it here," Nobu offered.

"I'm realizing now that the mirror might only work one way," Yuki said. "I've sat in front of her mirror doing my makeup a bunch of times and it's never opened. Maybe Shōnagon has to be there, or maybe there's a secret password or something."

The pheasant cocked its golden head and blinked its wide eyes. "Perhaps there is an answer in the prophecy."

"Which prophecy?" Nobu asked. "The master of divination issues prophecies every week."

"The prophecy about the contest," the pheasant said.

Nobu looked skeptical. "Are you sure such a thing exists?"

"The contest would not exist without a prophecy," the pheasant said.

"That's true," Nobu said. "Nobody makes decisions in the

palace without a prophecy to back them up. We could check the archive."

"How do we look for the prophecy without setting off the screaming lanterns?" Yuki asked.

Nobu shifted his gaze out the window. The lines in his forehead deepened as he pondered. "We could try patching the holes," he said. "If the lanterns can't open their eyes or their mouths, they can't see us and scream."

"Touching the lanterns won't wake them up?" Yuki asked.

"It might," Nobu said. "If one starts screaming, then we run back to the crawl space."

Doing something seemed better than sitting in the stall and doing nothing. "It's worth a try," Yuki said. "What do we patch them with?"

"I have some paper and a brush," Nobu said, opening a writing box that rested on a crate in the corner. "But we'll need a jar of pine resin to make the paper stick. The ladies would have used some while making the contest displays."

"We could ask Izumi to bring it out to us," Yuki suggested.

Nobu nodded. "Yes, that's much better than me trying to sneak in," he said, quickly grinding an ink stick and making ink. "'Izumi,'" he said as he wrote. "'We are going on a mission and need your help. Please leave a jar of pine resin on the veranda outside the door.'"

Nobu tucked some paper and an ink brush in his cloak while Yuki took off all but one of her robes so that she could move more freely. As they set out to deliver the message to Izumi, the pheasant flew alongside them in short bursts, landing on rails and branches. They briefly stopped at a shed where Nobu took a net attached to a bamboo pole. Approaching the garden gate, they saw two guards posted.

"I will make them chase me," the pheasant promised. Sure enough, when the pheasant strutted past them, the guards pointed and took off in pursuit.

In the garden, Yuki heard string music and chatter coming from the emperor's quarters. The gentlemen seemed to not have a care in the world. But the consort's quarters were quiet. Yuki wondered what had become of Jun. Had the guards caught her, or was she still skulking around the palace grounds? The pheasant glided past them and landed on the wisteria arbor. Nobu chose a path that cut through the spring quadrant. When they neared the empress's wing, they ducked behind a sculpted tree. Lamps flickered behind the lowered blinds. Otherwise, the party seemed to be over. Nobu darted up to the veranda while Yuki and the pheasant waited in the shadows.

After a servant opened the door and took the letter from Nobu, minutes passed with no response. Finally, the door cracked open again and Nobu spoke to the person on the other side. He returned to the garden looking miffed.

"The servant says Izumi told her not to wait for a response," he said.

"Does that mean she's not going to help us?" Yuki said, outraged. "Why would Izumi do that?"

"She might be attending the empress," Nobu said. "Or

Shōnagon might be watching her. It could mean many things."

"In this case, it means you're not going on a mission without me," Izumi announced, coming up behind them and handing Nobu a fabric satchel containing a jar of pine resin. "What happened? Shōnagon came back looking very upset and asked if I had seen you. Then she went to see Murasaki, of all people."

Yuki felt a teary wave of relief. "I'll tell you on the way to the archive," she said.

To avoid any guards posted at the garden's west gate, Nobu led them along the covered walkway to the aviary. The pheasant continued to half run, half fly alongside them.

"Is that the empress's pheasant?" Izumi asked.

The pheasant landed on the rail and cocked its head at her. "Hello," the bird said.

"The bird said hello!" Izumi exclaimed.

"Oh, good," Yuki said. "We can all hear it."

Yuki then related what had happened that evening. Izumi looked distraught.

"I think I might be sick," Izumi said. "I'm horrified beyond words. I didn't know, Yuki. Honestly, I didn't."

"I know," Yuki said, squeezing her hand. "Of course you didn't. None of this is your fault."

"But I was part of the contest," Izumi said, a haunted look entering her eyes. "This whole time I have been getting girls ready to become ghosts and outcasts."

"It's a terrible thing, but it's not your fault," Nobu said. "Right now, we need to focus on trying to help Yuki."

When they reached the secret entrance to the archive, Nobu removed the panel to the crawl space. While he lit the lamp inside, Izumi stripped off her outer layers as Yuki had. The pheasant pecked at the ground and gobbled up an insect. Then they all followed Nobu through the crawl space. After removing the loose floorboards, Nobu popped through the opening. Yuki handed him the net and the satchel. Then she stepped onto the stool and grabbed his hand. She worried less this time about having sweaty palms or getting stuck like Winnie-the-Pooh in the hole at Rabbit's house. Nobu helped Izumi up. The pheasant also fluttered through the opening.

Nobu studied the round paper lantern that hovered overhead. "Should we try patching this one first? That way if it screams, we don't have far to run," he said.

"Good idea," Izumi said.

Yuki held her breath as Nobu snared the floating lantern in the net, but the rips in the paper did not transform into two eyes and a mouth. While Nobu held the lantern on the floor, Yuki ripped up a piece of paper and brushed the edges with pine resin. Then Izumi used the sticky pieces as bandages over the rips. Once all three areas had been patched, Nobu released the lantern, which floated toward the ceiling. The three of them moved next to the opening, ready to jump into the crawl space. Using its beak, the pheasant pulled a scroll off the lowest shelf. The three patches seemed to stretch, as if the lantern had been awakened by the movement of the scroll, but no sound came out.

Breathing a sigh of relief, Yuki took a random scroll off a shelf. "This looks like a supply list," she said.

Izumi pulled a scroll from a different shelf. "This is a decree about the style of hat that a gentleman can wear to court."

"And this one is a letter to the emperor from a provincial governor," Nobu said.

They checked more scrolls along the row and continued to find a mix of documents.

"Why are they all thrown together?" Izumi said, frowning. "It's not much of a system. How would you ever find anything? We have a better chance of leaning a ladder against a cloud than we do of finding a single prophecy in the archive."

"The documents must be organized in some way," Yuki said. "Or maybe the prophecies are all kept together in one place."

Yuki walked to the end of the row and checked the sides of the shelving units for labels. Looking up and down the rows, she saw no signs posted. Then goose bumps rose on her arms. The last time they came to the archive, Yuki had counted eight rows. Now there were nine.

"Come look at this," she said. The new row had been added to the back of the room. The shelves were empty and the lighting dim because there was no lantern on patrol yet. "This has been added since we were last here."

"How odd," Nobu said.

"Nobu, have you ever noticed a new row added to the archive before?" Izumi asked.

"No, but I don't usually walk around," Nobu said. "I stay close to the opening just in case someone comes in."

The lack of a filing system gnawed at Yuki. It didn't make sense that the chamberlain—who had to be a very organized person to be put in charge of keeping the royal calendar and saving the imperial documents—had decided to throw the scrolls on the shelves all jumbled up like this. There had to be a reason.

"There are eight high priestesses," Izumi said. "Yuki would be the ninth and she was supposed to be initiated today. Do you think there's a connection between that and the number of rows?"

"That's it," Yuki said, moving back toward the hole in the floor. She gazed up, looking for the coppery glimmer that had caught her eye on the last visit. It was all coming together. The glittery edge was like the metallic ooze that had come out of Amaterasu's mirror. The master of divination had instructed her to roll up her reflection after she finished cutting. That's why the pheasant had called it the scrolling. "Pheasant, can you fly up and take down the scroll with the shiny edge?" she asked.

"Yes, of course," the pheasant said. The bird beat its wings, hovered next to the coppery scroll, and tugged on the edge with its talons. The scroll tumbled to the floor, partially unrolling. A girl with dark faraway eyes, tiny ears, and a heart-shaped face stared up at them blankly.

Izumi gasped. "That's a former high priestess," she said.

"But why mix her reflection in with all these letters?" Nobu asked.

"I'm not sure," Yuki said. "They're trying to hide it, I think. I'm wondering if that's why the rest of the papers aren't organized, because those documents don't matter. The chamberlain will never need to search for that decree about hats or the letter from the provincial governor. The other scrolls are only here to make this one hard to find if you don't know what you're looking for."

"That makes sense in a strange way," Izumi said.

"There should be one reflection in each row, then," Nobu said.

Yuki rolled up the scroll and placed it inside the fabric satchel that Izumi had used to carry the pine resin. Row by row, they patched the lanterns and retrieved each high priestess's reflection. They did the first row last. By then they were running low on pine resin. Yuki bit her lip as Nobu released the lantern, which strained around the mouth. But the bandage held. The last scroll revealed a girl with a long, narrow face and a brash expression.

"My friend," the pheasant said sadly.

Yuki patted the pheasant on the back and then packed the scroll in the satchel.

"That takes care of all the priestesses," Izumi said. "But the contest prophecy could be anywhere."

They walked through the archive row by row, scanning the shelves, without seeing a scroll that looked more important than the others. When they returned to the first row, Nobu leaned against the wall dejectedly. Izumi kept obsessively checking scrolls, even though she'd been the one to point out there was almost no chance of finding it that way.

"Pheasant, ask your friend the crow where the prophecy is," Nobu said, gesturing to the painting by the door.

The pheasant puffed out its wings. "The crow is not my friend," the bird said. "Yuki is my friend. And now you are my friend and Izumi is my friend."

"Thank you, pheasant," Nobu said with a grin. "I'm glad to have you as a friend. One can never have too many friends in the palace."

"Since it turns out you never know which ones are actually your friends," Yuki added darkly. She studied the painting, which hung from a large wooden rod. In the bottom right corner, two court ladies appeared to be laughing as they watched a crow chase a rabbit across the sky.

"What is happening here?" Yuki asked. "Why is the rabbit in the air?"

"The crow is associated with the sun and the rabbit symbolizes the moon," Nobu explained. "I think the sun is pushing the moon out of the sky."

"Shōnagon told me that the crack in the sky appeared because the former emperor was worshipping the moon god," Yuki said. "That can't be a coincidence."

Yuki pulled the bottom of the painting away from the wall but found nothing hidden behind it or on the back side.

Izumi turned away from the shelves and frowned at the scroll. "It is a very odd picture," she said.

"If the whole purpose of the archive is to hide the priest-esses' reflections, then perhaps the picture is a clue," Nobu said. "A crow chasing a rabbit isn't funny. So why are the ladies laughing?"

The master of divination loved jokes and riddles. Could the two ladies in the corner of the painting be laughing at a joke? Yuki tested out different variations: "Why did the moon run away from the sun? Why did the sun chase the moon?"

"Are you really trying to guess the spell?" Izumi said. "We'll be here all night."

"Looking at each piece of paper on the shelves will take more than a night," Nobu pointed out. "That would take days."

Days. Maybe the punchline had something to do with night and day. "What did the sun say to the moon? 'Time to leave. It's your day off,'" Yuki said.

The colors in the painting blurred and dissolved. A lengthy piece of text appeared.

"You did it!" Nobu exclaimed, rushing to her side.

"How did you do that?" Izumi said, astounded.

"I've heard a lot of these kinds of jokes," Yuki said.

"What is a joke?" asked the pheasant, who had perched behind them on a shelf at shoulder height.

"It's when you say something funny to make others laugh," Yuki explained.

"But nobody laughed," the bird said. "That means this joke is not funny."

"I know, pheasant," Yuki said. "Trust me, I know."

Nobu read the first line aloud. "'From the ashes of Mount Osore, we, the *itako*, do give to thee, the master of divination, two magic mirrors.'"

"Mount Osore is the gateway to the underworld," Izumi said. "The *itako* are blind mediums."

"The magic mirrors must be the ones that belong to Shōnagon and Murasaki," Yuki said.

Nobu continued reading:

Through the mirrors, two poets will come.
Hear their words and select the very best one.
The winner must cut her reflection
And willingly offer her memories to the sun.
In return, Amaterasu will heal the sky.
When one scroll weakens, more poets will vie
To be the next priestess on high.
But lock the scrolls and hide them all.
If reunited, the heavens will fall
And destroy the wicked in the capital.

None of them spoke as they all silently reread the prophecy.

"So the scrolling is reversible," Yuki said. "But if I give the priestesses their reflections, the sky falls. And if I don't scroll myself, the sky falls. Either way, your world is destroyed." Yuki was trapped, just like Murasaki and Shōnagon were.

"How can the sun goddess be so unfair?" Izumi cried.

"There must be a way," Nobu said, a note of desperation in his voice.

"I don't think there is," Yuki said. "To save you, I have to scroll myself."

The pheasant's head drooped. "My friend," the bird said softly.

It wasn't fair. Yuki had won the contest. People liked her here. She had finally made great friends. And it had all been for nothing.

Nobu eyed the enchanted lantern, which was shaking and jerking around in an effort to remove the bandages. The paper that they'd glued over its mouth had started to peel at one edge. "I don't know how much longer the glue will hold on this one," Nobu said. "I think we should go back to the stable and take the scrolls with us while we figure out what to do."

"Should we take the prophecy, too?" Izumi asked.

"That's a good idea," Yuki said.

As Nobu removed the wooden rod from the wall, Yuki heard a ripping noise. Turning around, she saw one eye patch on the lantern had torn. A black eye spiraled beneath the ripped paper.

"The lantern," Yuki called out. "It's awake."

Nobu hurriedly rolled up the prophecy as the second eye patch popped. "Run!" he shouted as the mouth patch broke and a high-pitched whistle pierced the air.

The pheasant flew down the aisle. Nobu sprinted after the bird, the prophecy tucked under his arm. Clutching the satchel of scrolls to her chest, Yuki ran as fast as she could. The lantern scream was unbearably shrill, a needle in her brain. As they turned into the row with the hole in the floor, Yuki caught a glimpse of Izumi's panicked face behind her while the lantern loomed over them like a drunken pirate. Then a long pink tongue shot from its mouth and Yuki shrieked.

Nobu reached the crawl space first and dropped the prophecy into the hole. Then he grabbed Izumi's hand and helped her inside. Yuki tossed the satchel on top of the prophecy. As she swung her legs into the opening, the lantern's tongue grabbed Nobu around the waist and started to drag him away.

"No!" Yuki shouted as she looked around for something to hit the lantern with. But the pheasant attacked first, pecking the pink tongue until the lantern recoiled and released Nobu. Yuki dropped into the crawl space, followed by the pheasant and Nobu, who pulled the floorboards overhead.

Izumi, covered in dust, was holding the lamp and breathing heavily. The pheasant's feathers looked ruffled and blood dripped from its beak. As the lantern jiggled the floorboards with its tongue, Nobu wiped the blood splatters from his forehead.

"Thank you, pheasant," he said. "Let's go quickly before the guards get here."

Nobu picked up the prophecy while Yuki grabbed the satchel. Then they all scurried toward the loose panel. When they reached the opening, Nobu blew out the lamp and looked outside carefully. After raising his index finger to his lips, he pointed in the direction he thought they should go. Keeping to the shadows, they skulked along the path. The screaming lantern had left Yuki with an angry ringing in her ears.

Nobu led them up the stairs to the veranda of a building between the archive and the Purple Sanctum. From the veranda, Yuki could see guards streaming into the entrance of the chamberlain's and the master of divination's offices. Nobu took them through a covered walkway. Then they hurried down a short flight of stairs and cut through a small, enclosed garden.

"Pheasant," Nobu said, "we're going to go through the emperor's quarters. We'll meet you on the other side."

If the pheasant said anything in response, Yuki couldn't hear it. She hoped her eardrums hadn't burst. The bird flew up to the roof and disappeared.

"Hold your fans up to your faces," Nobu said. "I'll take the scrolls and the prophecy, since they aren't looking for me."

"Nobu, what are you thinking?" Izumi hissed. "We can't walk through the emperor's quarters."

"It's safer than crossing through the main courtyard, where there's nowhere to hide from the guards," Nobu said.

"But Yuki and I aren't properly dressed," Izumi said,

gesturing at her single robe. "Everyone will notice us."

"The more people who are around, the less likely they are to take notice," Nobu said. "I'll walk ahead of you. Follow my cues and stay behind pillars and screens as much as possible."

Yuki opened her fan. Nobu slipped through the first door and motioned for them to follow. The gallery was bustling with servants and courtiers. First, she and Izumi hid behind a pillar. Then they moved behind a screen. Yuki felt like a spy in a movie. As they moved behind the next pillar, Izumi whispered to Yuki to slow down.

"Ladies never walk quickly," she said.

When they reached the reception area, Nobu ducked behind a portable curtain. Yuki counted to five between each step she took. After what felt like an eternity, they joined him.

"We're going to go straight across," Nobu whispered, pulling his cap low on his forehead. "Don't rush. That will only draw attention to you."

"That's what I just told her," Izumi said.

Nobu stepped out from behind the curtain. As Yuki started to stand, he immediately dropped down and held out his hand to say "wait." Yuki exchanged a wide-eyed glance with Izumi.

"The guards think a mouse must have set off the screaming lantern," a man said. "The door was locked and they didn't find anyone inside."

"A mouse creates a disturbance in the archive on the same night that our high priestess runs away? Impossible."

Yuki recognized the regent's gravelly voice and a shiver went down her spine.

"Keep looking for her," the regent said. "Make sure there's a guard at every point of entry to Empress Teishi's quarters."

"Yes, sir."

Once they heard footsteps retreating, Nobu peeked out. He motioned for them to follow him. Thankfully a group of courtiers had gathered between them and the emperor's dais, and nobody paid any attention to them. They had almost reached the other side of the reception hall when a gentleman called out to Nobu.

"Page boy!"

With the satchel and prophecy tucked under his arm, Nobu turned to speak to the courtier with his usual attentiveness, as if nothing was out of the ordinary. Yuki and Izumi kept walking toward the next pillar. Yuki's heart was beating faster than a hummingbird's wings.

"Page boy, please deliver this message to the head of the guards at once," the courtier said.

"Right away, sir," Nobu said.

When Nobu passed the pillar where they were hiding, he dropped the note inside a vase and said with an impish smile, "Lucky for us, the head of the guards is very busy right now."

They continued to dodge servants and courtiers as they made their way to the other end of the gallery. Yuki felt like she was running the mile in PE class. It was either never going to end or she was going to throw up or both. Finally, they exited the emperor's quarters and reached the quiet side of the palace. The pheasant was waiting for them at the stable door. Yuki had never been so grateful to smell ox poop. She hoped for a moment that she would wake up and find herself with her head down on a desk at Juana Maria Middle School while the scent of manure drifted through the windows from the neighboring farm fields.

"Do you think the guards will look for me here?" Yuki asked Nobu as he closed the barn door behind them. "I don't want you and Izumi to get in trouble on my account."

"It's too late for that," Izumi said.

"I should say so," said a voice that did not belong to Nobu or Izumi.

Yuki whirled around. A figure stepped out of the empty stall and held up a lamp. It was Shōnagon.

14

Throwing the Dragon, Part 2

The same ox that had nuzzled Yuki earlier stuck its head into the aisle and lowed. Shōnagon, dressed in the simpler, less showy robes of a servant, placed her hand between its sugary-brown eyes.

"I do love an ox with a small forehead," Shōnagon declared. "I will have to add that to my list of things that are pleasing."

Nobu reached for the door, his eyebrows raised in a question mark. He thought they should run. But where? Yuki was worn out from evading lanterns and guards and courtiers. There was nowhere else to hide in the palace. To avoid the scrolling, she would have to persuade Shōnagon not to turn her in. Yuki shook her head and Nobu lowered his hand.

"You took the reflections from the archive," Shōnagon said, eyeing the satchel. "That is most impressive. I'm sure you have many questions at this point. And of course, I must apologize."

Yuki wanted to say something withering that would put Shōnagon in her place. She wanted to see Shōnagon burst into tears and beg for forgiveness. Instead, her heart began to pound louder and louder, faster and faster, and the words swirled so quickly around her brain that she couldn't speak.

"You were going to let them decapitate Yuki," Izumi said accusingly. "And you lied to me! The high priestesses are all locked up here in the palace. How could you?"

Yuki was grateful that Izumi was speaking for her. Shōnagon shielded her eyes with her hand. Her chest heaved. "Yes, to save our world, I was going to sacrifice Yuki," she admitted. "Yuki, I am genuinely fond of you. I am not proud to be part of this terrible conspiracy. I am sorry."

"You need to tell us everything," Nobu said, his eyes flashing with anger. "We have to find a way to free the priestesses and save Yuki."

Taking the prophecy and the scrolls, he set them on the floor inside the empty stall. Then he spread out more ox blankets for them all to kneel on. Shōnagon played with the tassel on her closed fan and kept her eyes cast on the ground. Yuki sat between Nobu and Izumi. The pheasant nestled by her side.

"My goodness, is that the empress's golden pheasant? What *haven't* you found this evening?" Shōnagon said with a nervous laugh.

Izumi unrolled all eight reflections in the center of their circle. "Never mind about the pheasant," she said. "These girls need your help. Yuki needs your help."

Shōnagon looked down at the ground again and nodded. "When I first told you about the contest, I left out several important details," she said. "The regent himself accompanied the master of divination to Mount Osore. Upon learning that the winning poet would have to be sacrificed to appease Amaterasu, he immediately realized that the families of those girls would seek revenge if they learned their daughters had been decapitated. So he asked the witches for a way to bring contestants from another time, girls who had no ties here, without families to demand justice. That is how he came into possession of two magic mirrors, one for me and one for Murasaki. Each of us received the mirror through a trusted confidant, and we were led to believe this would give us an advantage in the contest. Neither of us were told that the other had a magic mirror. I was also warned that if anyone found out where my contestants came from, including the empress or any of the attendants, the punishment would be decapitation. Even though I trust Izumi completely, I was terrified when she witnessed the arrival of a contestant. But, of course, she has been the model of discretion."

"But the prophecy says you have to scroll yourself willingly," Yuki pointed out. "You weren't actually at risk of decapitation."

"That is what Amaterasu requires of the young poets sacrificed through *her* mirror," Shōnagon said. "The master of divination has his own special mirror for run-of-the-mill decapitations, and in those cases, willingness does not matter. Especially if the blade of a sword is at the back of one's neck."

"You went to visit our contestants at the temple after they won," Izumi said. "Was that a lie, too?"

"Not at first," Shōnagon said. "Even though I saw the scrolling with my own eyes, I did not believe the girls had their memories drained. That didn't make sense. How could they perform their daily rites if they had been decapitated? On my visits, I would be taken to a mountain temple. But I would never see the high priestess during my stay. Notes would arrive with various excuses. The third time this happened, I barged my way into her quarters and found only an elderly lady, a relative of the regent, who took care of the temple. She was the one sending the messages. I was utterly confounded, yet I was in no position to confront the regent. Murasaki had her own suspicions, and as we came to trust each other over time, we pieced together what was happening."

"Did Murasaki make sure Jun lost so that you wouldn't be decapitated?" Yuki knew she shouldn't care if she had won fair and square. There were bigger things at stake. But she had to know.

"Absolutely not," Shōnagon declared. "The outcome is beyond our control. The poets the mirrors send are extremely talented and determined to win. Besides, one never knows what will move the judges."

"If the winners are locked up in Destiny Hall, what does the regent do with the losers?" Nobu asked.

"I believe they are sent to the Tedium," Shōnagon said.

Izumi and Nobu looked stunned. "Are the losers at least kept together in the Tedium?" Nobu asked.

"I don't know," Shōnagon said, tugging on the tassel of her fan again. "Perhaps I have not wanted to know."

Looking back, Yuki realized Shōnagon had said something vague about the losers not being allowed to stay. Yuki had jumped to the conclusion that that meant they went back through the mirror. Now the conversation that Yuki had overheard between Murasaki and Shōnagon in the orange grove made more sense.

"You made me believe the losers got to go home," Yuki said. "Is that even possible? Can a contestant go home through your mirror?"

Shōnagon's chin dipped to her chest and she folded her arms. She looked miserable. "I don't know that, either," she said. "I don't think so. On occasion, a girl would change her mind in the middle of the contest and would ask the mirror to open and take her home. None were successful."

Even though Yuki had been prepared to be the high priestess, she was stunned. She thought that after her powers waned and the next high priestess was selected, she would have the option to go home if she wanted. Was she really stuck in the mirror world forever? Yuki looked at the reflections of each high priestess fanned out on the floor. Probably all of them had come here looking for a fresh start. Like her, they had all aspired to do something bigger, something important.

"What if we can get hold of Amaterasu's mirror and I make a new deal with the goddess?" Yuki asked. "Like, what if we restored the memories to all the high priestesses and then we actually did live in a temple and wrote poems in her honor every day?"

Shōnagon's eyes lit up. "Did you see Amaterasu in the mirror, then?" she asked. "I wondered what it was you saw earlier that made you run. I hoped there might be something that would give us a path forward."

Yuki frowned. "I didn't see the goddess," she said. "Only my own memories. But if her essence is in the mirror, maybe she can hear me."

"Perhaps," Shōnagon said, but she sounded doubtful. "We would have to tell the master of divination that you had changed your mind about the ceremony in order for you to look into Amaterasu's mirror again. You wouldn't have much time, since he would be standing there making sure you scroll your reflection."

"I have to try," Yuki said. "What other choice do I have?"

In the open window, the dawn sky was awash in pinks and purples. This might be the last time Yuki would ever see the crow chase the rabbit out of the sky.

Nobu leaned over to reread the prophecy. "I think there is one other possibility that would allow Yuki and the priestesses to keep their reflections," he said. "I notice the prophecy says that the heavens will fall over the wicked in the capital."

"We know that already," Izumi said.

"Let me finish," he said. "The prophecy doesn't say over the *whole* empire. Only the wicked in the capital. Not everyone in the capital is wicked. Some of us might be spared. If Amaterasu refuses Yuki's request, we might have time to escape. All of us, including Yuki and the eight priestesses."

"And let our beautiful capital be destroyed?" Izumi said with horror. "How can you suggest such a thing? I don't want Yuki to sacrifice herself, either. But where would we live if the capital is gone?"

"My mother has a cousin who is an official in Dazaifu," Nobu said. "It's a big port city. If we can find a ship, we can go there."

"If the regent survives, you know he will immediately order the clan that controls the province to turn us in," Izumi said. "We will all be decapitated."

Nobu's ears turned pink. "You're right," he said. "It was a stupid idea."

"Wait, now, while I think about this," Shōnagon said. "Nobu is right to focus on that line of the prophecy. Surely our great goddess would spare those who are good at heart. Why else mention the wicked? But Izumi is also right to point out that any man looking to take power, whether the regent or the head of a provincial clan, might make a great show out of capturing Yuki and the eight priestesses and claiming that scrolling them will restore order. That is why you must go to a place where they won't dare come after you. You must escape to the Tedium."

Nobu and Izumi both recoiled. "What?" Izumi said incredulously. "How is living among ogres and demons safer than going to the other provinces?"

"Remember what I told you about the priest who said that the Tedium is no more dangerous than any other place in the empire?" Shōnagon said. "He claimed that the people who have been banished there are happy to keep these tall tales alive as a measure of self-protection. They don't want anyone coming after them. They want to be left alone. I did not believe this priest at the time, but he spoke with great sincerity."

Something else was nagging at Yuki. "Shōnagon, are you not coming with us?" she asked.

Shōnagon raised her hands and gave them a rueful smile. "That will be up to Amaterasu," she said. "I have done my share of wicked things thanks to this contest."

Despair roiled across Izumi's face. Nobu sucked in his cheeks. Yuki waited for one of them to speak.

"One thing I've learned from living in the stable is that it is my friends who bring me happiness, not the palace," Nobu said. "If it means Yuki will not have to scroll herself and we can all be together, then I will go to the Tedium."

"I agree," Yuki said. "All we need is paper and ink and each other."

Tears welled in Izumi's eyes. Yuki had only lived in the palace for a short time, but she understood the grief that Izumi must feel saying goodbye to a life of beauty and learning and leisure.

"Fine, I'll go," Izumi said.

The pheasant, who had left Yuki's side to peck around the corner of the stall, lifted its golden head. "I wish to stay with my friends," the bird said. "I will go, too."

"The pheasant can speak!" Shōnagon exclaimed.

222

"You've made a lot of new friends tonight," Yuki said to the pheasant. "All right. So the plan is, I'll ask Amaterasu to let all the priestesses go without breaking the sky. If I can't find her or if she says no, then we leave for the Tedium. How are we going to do that, though? Won't the master of divination call the guards?"

"I will distract the guards," the pheasant promised.

Nobu grinned. "You're very good at that," he said. "I will ask the ox drivers to get two carriages ready."

"To end the contest once and for all, we must also include Murasaki in our plan," Shōnagon said.

"Why would Murasaki help?" Izumi asked. "Isn't it in her interest for Yuki to scroll herself?"

"Murasaki is as tired of this contest as I am," Shōnagon said. "For this to be truly over, both of us must destroy our mirrors. I believe we can trust her."

Shōnagon took off her outer layer. "Izumi, you can wear this servant's robe so that no one will stop you," she said. "I need you to go to my room and bring my mirror. Nobu, I am going to write a note for Murasaki that you must deliver to her. Then you and Izumi should find each other and wait for us near Destiny Hall. Yuki, I think we should try to speak with the other priestesses and let them know about our plan before calling for the master of divination. We may need to move quickly and there won't be time for explanations."

While Izumi put on the servant's robe, Yuki pulled on the teal outer robe that she'd worn earlier to the initiation ceremony and returned the reflections to the satchel. After

223

Shōnagon had scribbled a note for Murasaki, they all left the stable together. Nobu and Izumi headed for the living quarters while Yuki, Shōnagon, and the pheasant made their way to Destiny Hall. The dawn sky no longer looked like sky, but like the parched earth along the San Andreas fault line. Yuki tried to be angry with Shōnagon but couldn't. All she felt was blank inside, like the summit of the snow mountain. Something near but distant.

As they approached the guards in front of Destiny Hall, Shōnagon steeled her shoulders and put on an imperious face.

"I've found the new high priestess and she's had a change of heart," Shōnagon announced. "She is now ready for her initiation."

The guards exchanged an uneasy glance. "I'm sorry, my lady, but the master of divination isn't here," one said. "We can't let you in."

"Nonsense," Shōnagon said. "He's been notified and will surely be here at any moment."

"You'll have to wait, my lady," he said.

"If the high priestess runs off again while we are standing outside, I can assure you that the master of divination will be cross indeed," Shōnagon said. "Your guard corps already allowed the other contestant to elude you. You will be in deep trouble if this one gets away, too."

The guards exchanged another uneasy glance. Then they stepped aside.

"Did they not catch Jun?" Yuki whispered as they hurried up the stairs.

"Oh, I have no idea," Shōnagon said. "But when you speak with authority, others tend to believe you."

The pheasant was waiting for them outside the double doors. Yuki tucked the satchel with the reflections under her left arm and scooped up the pheasant in her right arm, more for her own comfort. But the bird let her.

Inside the hall, Shōnagon lit a lamp and surveyed the room. Amaterasu's mirror had been put away and the standing screen had been moved to the side, revealing the painted door in full. A ferocious red demon with jagged shark teeth and an ear-to-ear grin faced forward, looking like it was charging the viewer. Rings of fire dotted the background.

They walked up to the demon door. Though the door did not appear to be locked, it didn't budge when Shōnagon tried to open it. "The master of divination must have placed an enchantment," she said.

The pheasant fluttered out of Yuki's arms to the floor. "Is it time for another joke?" the bird asked. "Please tell a funny one this time."

"What a noisy bird you are," Shōnagon said. "The painting might offer a clue. Perhaps it is from the springtime ritual when we drive away the evil spirits. Demon, out! Good fortune, in!"

The door remained shut. Shōnagon tried again. "Demon, out! Let us in!"

Still the door didn't listen. "Can I try?" Yuki asked. "Unfortunately, you have to think like the master of divination." *And Doug*, she thought.

"Why is the demon always angry?" Yuki said to the door. "Because he's hotheaded."

"Oh my," Shōnagon said. "Have you actually been paying attention to the master of divination?"

The door didn't move. Yuki tried again. "What did the medium say when she apologized to the exorcist? 'I'm sorry, I don't know what possessed me.'"

Shōnagon laughed with delight. "Well, that is much too clever for our dear master of divination," she said.

Yuki studied the painting. There were eight rings of fire, four on either side of the demon.

"Shōnagon, what do the flaming rings represent?" Yuki asked.

"Those are the Eight Great Hells," Shōnagon said.

That had to be a clue. She remembered a joke Doug once told about a depressed demon who walked into a bar. "Why did the demon quit working in the Eight Great Hells? Because it was a soul-crushing experience," Yuki said.

The panel door slid open. Shōnagon looked astonished. "I had no idea you had this in you," she said.

The pheasant emitted a whistling laugh. "I like that joke very much," the bird said, while Yuki silently thanked Doug.

Yuki and Shōnagon stepped tentatively into the dim room. At first Yuki thought they had unlocked the wrong chamber.

Scanning the depths, she saw no one inside. Then she heard a soft whisper that sounded like wind in the eaves.

"Have we reached a new century already?" a voice asked.

"We are the clan that does not wish to grow," another said. "Because that means another one has been scrolled."

Yuki looked up toward the ceiling and saw eight translucent forms floating in a semicircle. Before she could explain why they had come, the scrolls flew out of the satchel. Yuki tried to grab them, but she was too slow. Then the scrolls unfurled in the air, and each flew to its person. As reflections and faces reunited, white auras flashed. Then colors emerged, silk robes in teal and red. As they gained color, the priestesses descended until their feet reached the floor.

"I guess we'll find out how long it takes before the sky falls," Yuki said, letting the satchel drop to the floor.

"Oh dear," Shōnagon said with a nervous laugh. "That didn't go according to plan, did it?"

"I remember my name," said one.

"I am whole again," said another.

"Thank you for saving us," they all said.

In the lamplight, the priestesses looked at each other with startled eyes. Probably the memory of how they came to be locked behind the demon door had come flooding back. Then their eyes fell on Shōnagon.

"You knew," said one priestess. "You and Murasaki both."

Shōnagon bowed her head. "Yes, and I am sorry."

"Listen, we don't have much time," Yuki said. "Shōnagon is trying to help us. I'm going to ask Amaterasu to set us free and remove the curse on the sky. You have to be ready to leave at a moment's notice, though, if it doesn't work."

Her words were drowned out by the clatter of footsteps on the stairs. Yuki turned around to see the regent sweeping into Destiny Hall, looking like a dark wizard in his boxy black robe and tall black hat. The master of divination and the chamberlain flanked him. A dozen guards trailed in their wake. The regent stopped in front of the demon door, elbows out and fists on hips. The priestesses huddled around Yuki and Shōnagon.

"Shōnagon," the regent said. "I'm surprised to see you mixed up in this. Between you and Murasaki, I always took you to be the more pragmatic of the two. And Yuki from the Land of a Merry Cat. Never have we had a contestant quite so outspoken and meddlesome."

"Except for the ninja," the priestesses murmured.

"Even the ninja didn't find the scrolls," the regent said. "But I'm afraid your newfound memories will be short-lived. You will all be decapitated at once."

Through the open front door, Yuki saw the sky had turned an ominous green-gray, and the jagged lines had deepened. Three shadowy forms climbed the steps and entered the hall. Murasaki hurried toward them with Nobu and Izumi trailing her. Murasaki had changed out of her red contest robes and wore simple, plain robes the color of wheat.

"This game has gone on long enough," Murasaki said, her face smoldering with anger. "The mirror portals have been destroyed. There will be no more contestants. At least, not through us."

"Impossible," the regent scoffed.

"We thought you might say that," Murasaki said, displaying a mirror fragment on her palm. "Enchantments can be removed, you know."

Yuki wasn't sure if Murasaki was bluffing or not. Nobu might have given her the shards from the golden pheasant's cage. Still, Yuki felt bolstered by Murasaki's tactics. They were all fighting back.

The craggy lines around the regent's eyes deepened. "I will not let our capital be destroyed," he said. "I will go back to Mount Osore for new mirrors if I must. If you and Shōnagon think you can defy me and your literary reputations will protect you, then you are mistaken. We have many writers who would be happy to take your places at court."

While the regent spoke, Yuki noticed the guards had encircled them. They were trapped.

"Read the prophecy," Yuki said. "Amaterasu won't accept our reflections if they're taken against our will. You lied to us before, so we did the scrolling with our own hands. If you want to save the sky, you need to make a deal with us."

"You are in no position to bargain," the regent said, crossing his arms. But doubt had entered his eyes.

"Let us go to the temple where you pretended to send the priestesses and we'll perform the daily rites," Yuki said. "We'll ask Amaterasu to spare the capital."

"Do you take me for a fool?" the regent said. "Unless all nine of you scroll yourselves, I'll decapitate your friends one by one, starting with Shōnagon. Then Murasaki. Then Shōnagon's assistant and the page boy."

"You'd still be forcing us," Yuki argued. "Amaterasu won't accept our reflections unless we scroll ourselves willingly."

"I'll take that chance," the regent said.

Yuki had to think of a way to trick the regent, to make him think he was getting what he wanted. If he thought that she didn't want to scroll herself and she pretended to give in, then she'd have a chance to look into Amaterasu's mirror again. "I throw the dragon," Yuki said.

"Whatever do you mean by that?" the regent said indignantly.

"I throw the dragon," Yuki said. "I challenge you to a contest. A riddle contest. As the newest priestess, I still have my full powers. I'm the one you need. If you win, I'll scroll myself, and my friends get to leave. But if I win, you let us go to the temple and I promise to ask Amaterasu to reverse the prophecy. It's your only chance to survive."

The regent threw back his head and laughed. "Well, you are plucky," he said. After turning to look out the entrance at the sky, where fragments now hung like the loose ceiling tiles at school, he nodded. "I accept your challenge."

Nobu arranged four cushions and two writing tables in the center of the hall where Amaterasu's mirror had been earlier. The chamberlain brought them each a writing box and a stack of paper. Yuki chose Izumi to be her reader. The regent picked the master of divination. Yuki knelt behind their writing table with Izumi by her side and faced the regent. Shōnagon, Murasaki, Nobu, and the eight priestesses clustered behind her. Out of the corner of her eye, Yuki saw the pheasant peek its head around the folding screen. The chamberlain and the guards remained standing behind the regent. They were trying to intimidate her. But after beating Jun at poetry and figuring out the master of divination's passwords, Yuki was feeling calm and confident.

"You may go first," the regent said.

Yuki dipped her brush in the ink and then wrote out her first riddle with the answer at the bottom.

Izumi took the paper from her and read the question aloud: "I can hold your weight because I'm incredibly strong. But I can also bend down to the ground. What am I?"

"Bamboo," the regent said in a dismissive tone that made it clear he was not impressed with her opening shot. The regent picked up a brush, and words flowed effortlessly onto the page.

"I have no hands. But with my twin, I can pick things up," the master of divination said. "What am I?"

"A chopstick," Yuki said. She quickly wrote her next riddle on a clean sheet of paper and handed it to Izumi.

"I spark. But if you hold me in your hand, I don't burn," Izumi said. "What am I?"

"A firefly," the regent said, already writing. He was trying to make her feel unworthy. She tried not to let his mind games get to her.

The chamberlain read aloud, "I can be cast on the ground, but I never get hurt. What am I?"

"A shadow," Yuki said. She had planned to follow up with "I'm a room, but I have no doors or windows." Then she realized that was her brain thinking in English. The word *mushroom* in Japanese didn't incorporate *room*. The riddle wouldn't work.

Seeing her hesitate, the regent smirked. "Did you run out of riddles already?" he asked. "I suppose it's my own fault for not setting a time limit. Please take as long as you need."

Yuki wished she were writing poems, and that thought prompted a riddle.

"I can be measured and I have a form, but I can't wear clothes," Izumi said. "What am I?"

"You can't pose a riddle with the same answer as a previous riddle," the regent said with annoyance. "I'll let you go again."

"The answer isn't a shadow," Yuki said.

Finally, she'd thrown the regent off-balance. "That could be true of many things," he said. "Rice, for instance."

"Rice has a form, but measurement isn't part of its identity," Yuki said. "Are you choosing rice as your answer?"

"Or snow," the regent said. "There are many answers that could work."

A snowman could wear clothes. But Yuki kept that

thought to herself since she wanted to beat him. "It's a good thing we didn't set a time limit," she said.

The regent's eyes narrowed and his mouth formed a hard line. Yuki held her breath. She was on the brink of winning.

"The answer is a poem," he said.

She tried not to let her disappointment show. That had been her best shot. The regent handed his paper to the master of divination.

"I have a head of white hair when I am young and black hair as I grow old. What am I?"

Yuki stared at the edge of her mat. Her mind went blank. Was it some kind of doll or toy? Or maybe a sea creature? When she looked up, the regent was smirking.

"I don't know," Yuki admitted.

"The answer is an ink brush," the master of divination said. But he said it softly, with kindness. "It's settled, then. I will fetch the mirror."

Even though Yuki had a plan, even though she knew the regent was more likely to keep his word if she lost, she was devastated. She would not see Nobu or Izumi again. Yuki and the regent rose and bowed to each other.

"You may say your goodbyes," the regent said.

When she turned around, she saw despair on the priestesses' faces. Shōnagon and Murasaki stood with their heads bowed. Nobu's forehead creased with concern. He clutched the pheasant in his arms.

"I can't bear it," Izumi said with tears in her eyes. "I can't bear that the regent gets to win."

Yuki took Izumi's hand in hers. "I challenged the regent because he would never let you go otherwise," she said. "Also, I'm not going to scroll myself. I'm going to ask Amaterasu to keep you safe, and then I'm going to escape through the mirror and try to go home."

Yuki hadn't realized she was going to say that until the words came out. Home. She did want to go home.

"During the scrolling ceremony, the mirror surface became soft," Yuki said. "I think I can go through. But I'm going to need your help, pheasant."

The pheasant cocked its head and blinked its wide eyes. "Yes, I will always help my friend," the bird said.

"The master of divination is going to ask me to use a knife to cut around the edge of the mirror," Yuki said. "When I get about a quarter of the way around, can you attack whoever is standing closest to me? It will probably be the master of divination. But it might be the regent. I need a distraction so that I have time to go inside the mirror."

"Yes," the pheasant said. "What is a quarter?"

Timing would be everything. Maybe she could call out to the pheasant. But what if she got caught up in the memories as she cut the mirror and forgot to give the bird its cue?

"I think I need you to stay, too, Nobu," Yuki said. "I'm sorry."

Nobu nodded resolutely. "Whatever it is, I'll do it," he said.

"Can you stand close by and watch me as I cut?" Yuki asked. "Once I've gone about a quarter of the way around the mirror, can you call out to the pheasant?"

"Of course," Nobu said. "Pheasant, I will shout '*ken ken*,' and that is your signal to attack."

"Nobu, once I'm inside, I need you to break the mirror," Yuki said. "That way this can never happen again."

Nobu turned pale. "Break the sun goddess's mirror," he said.

Yuki had only been thinking about closing the portal for good. She hadn't stopped to think about what a big deal that would be, to destroy a sacred object that belonged to a deity.

Shōnagon took a step forward. "I will break the mirror," she said. "Nobu, once you have given the signal to the pheasant, you must take Murasaki, Izumi, and the priestesses to the carriages and leave. Don't wait for me. The bird and I will find you."

Yuki gave Shōnagon a grateful smile. Then she turned to Izumi. "Once you're settled in the Tedium, please try to find Jun and the other contestants," she said.

Izumi nodded. "I will. This is goodbye, then," she said, tears falling down her cheeks and streaking her powder.

"I'll never forget you," Yuki said, squeezing her hand. "And just think, you'll get to write every day with the other high priestesses."

"I'll miss you," Izumi said.

"I'll miss you, too," Yuki said.

235

Murasaki stood with a stiff, formal posture, but her face looked softer now. "You are bold and brave," she said, bowing to Yuki. "It has been an honor hearing your poetry and watching you compete."

"It's been my honor to be here at court with you and Shōnagon," Yuki said, bowing in return.

While Murasaki conferred with Shōnagon, Yuki turned to Nobu, who still held the pheasant in his arms. "I guess I should say goodbye to you both now, while I have the chance," she said, suddenly feeling awkward.

"Goodbye, my friend," the bird said, bobbing its golden head.

"Perhaps we will meet again in our dreams," Nobu said.

During their study sessions for the contest, Izumi had read her several poems about people who shared a strong bond meeting in the dream space. If Yuki believed it, maybe it could come true. "I hope so," she said.

When the regent announced that they had wasted enough time, the guards ushered Murasaki, Izumi, and the eight priestesses outside and slid the doors closed. Yuki was worried that the regent might send Nobu away. But Nobu quickly busied himself by lighting more candles. As a page boy doing his duties, he became invisible to the men.

"Yuki, you have been a most outstanding protégé," Shōnagon said. "I am truly sorry that you will not serve as high priestess here. But I am certain that your poetic gifts will lead you to greatness in any world you choose to inhabit."

"I will put you at the top of my list of most splendid teach-ers," Yuki said.

"The gift of immortality is all I ask," Shōnagon said with a wry smile.

The master of divination set Amaterasu's mirror on the low table. As Yuki knelt before the mirror, the chamber-lain brought out the knife on a silver tray. She picked up the knife. Her solemn face stared back at her in the reflection.

Amaterasu, if you can hear me, please let my friends escape and let this contest come to an end, she thought.

But the mirror's surface didn't change. In the reflection, Yuki still saw her face, which now had a hint of desperation. She also saw Shōnagon standing stoically behind her to the left and the regent watching her like a hawk to the right. Nobu had already slipped over to the front door.

"You may unsheathe the knife," the master of divination said.

Yuki concentrated hard on the mirror, praying that Ama-terasu would reveal herself somehow. But there was still no sign. Yuki's hands trembled as she removed the cover from the blade.

"Gaze into the mirror," the master of divination said. "Starting from the top, run the blade around the edge. Once you have gone all the way around, peel off your reflection, roll it up, and say, 'I place my art in the service of the great goddess Amaterasu.'"

Yuki pressed the knife tip into the top of the mirror at

twelve o'clock. A thick bronze dot welled up as the blade pierced the surface. As Yuki dragged the knife around the edge, her reflection clouded over and then cleared. She saw her mother in a swimming pool holding out her hands as Yuki's two-year-old self let go of the wall and lunged forward in the water. The scene was so vivid, she could smell the chlorine.

She kept cutting.

Yuki looked down at her feet, encased in fleecy pajamas. She was bouncing up and down as her father dandled her on his knee, pretending to be a horse.

She ran through the sprinklers with Julio, the water shockingly cold.

She stood at the microphone in the elementary school auditorium, about to spell *epidemiology* and win the spelling bee.

Nearing the quarter mark, Yuki fought to keep her mind present, to not get caught in the memories.

She was lying in bed on the eve of her father's burial and worrying that he would be lonely in the cemetery by himself. She was standing in their living room in the Valley amid the moving boxes, crushed by the knowledge that she was leaving her childhood behind.

Yuki was so absorbed, she barely heard Nobu shout, "*Ken ken!*" His voice sounded far away. She tore herself away from the memories. She forced herself to close her eyes.

"Page boy, what are you doing?" the regent thundered.

Yuki heard beating wings and an angry squawk. Opening

her eyes, she saw a flurry of gold feathers above the mirror. The master of divination flailed his arms and stumbled around as the pheasant attacked. The regent came around the table to try to get the bird. This was her chance. Yuki threw off her robe, stuck the knife in the waistband of her trouser skirt, and pressed on the mirror's surface with both hands.

"Please, great goddess, let me go home," she said.

Tiny waves rippled across the reflection, growing in intensity until the mirror expanded to the size of a wheel on a semitruck. Amaterasu was listening after all. Yuki stepped onto the table and scrambled through the opening into a cool, watery tunnel. Last time, Yuki had seen Shōnagon beckoning from the other end. But inside Amaterasu's mirror, the tunnel had no end in sight.

Pausing to look over her shoulder, Yuki saw the room spin. Shōnagon must have hurled the mirror to the floor. Was it broken? Yuki couldn't tell. The other side of the mirror was dark and murky, with a flickering around the edges from the candlelight. Yuki prayed that Shōnagon, Nobu, and the pheasant would not get hurt protecting her. She hoped they would all find a true sanctuary in the Tedium. Then she took off running down the tunnel.

Like before, the air was syrupy, and after only a few steps her breathing was labored. Then she had a choice to make. The tunnel suddenly spoked into what seemed like an infinite number of pathways. She picked one at random. Soon blurry figures bobbed up ahead. Her father came into focus, carrying a tray with a chocolate cake in the shape of a lion—two large cake rounds for the head and body, cupcakes for the ears and paws, and a red licorice mane. Seven candles blazed on the cake while kids from her first-grade class crowded around the table, singing "Happy Birthday." She wanted to fling her arms around her father's neck and crush the cake between them and never let go. But her seven-year-old self was reveling in being the center of attention.

Please let me have a puppy, she thought as her father set the lion cake in front of her.

These better not be trick candles, she thought, taking a deep breath and preparing to blow them out.

Julio and the other kids chanted, "Are you one? Are you two? Are you three?"

You are not seven, Yuki reminded herself. *You are inside the mirror, trying to go home.* It was like being in a dream and suddenly realizing you are dreaming. She pulled out of her seven-year-old self and the party blurred.

Yuki moved through the tunnel, half running, half swimming. Again, she was faced with more branching tunnels. Her father would have loved the buffet of choices and probably would have moved randomly through the passages. But Yuki thought her mother would make a plan, like choosing every third tunnel on the left. Neither parent's approach was helping her in the moment, though.

When she had come through Shōnagon's mirror, all the

240

memories had been painful. But what if they hadn't been random? What if they had been reflections of her state of mind? She'd felt abandoned by her mother and Julio and her father. And so she had turned to moments that would make her want to run away. Maybe the reverse was also true. If she wanted to go home badly enough, maybe she could find a way through her memories to present-day Julio. That meant she needed to find her twelve-year-old self.

She took off down a passageway and spotted herself at age four at her butterfly-themed birthday party. Veering away, she chose another branch, where she saw herself at age six opening a Christmas gift from her grandmother in Japan that had all kinds of cool origami paper and stationery. At least she was getting older. She kept running until she saw her mother holding up a photo book from when she was ten.

She ran toward that image. Suddenly she was in her ten-year-old self, sitting with her mother on the couch with a photo book on her lap. The title read "The Real Story of Trudy the Tiger" by Yuki Snow. After Yuki had discovered that almost none of her writing had been included in the fifth-grade book project to raise money for endangered species, she had come home and cried. So Hana had found Yuki's submissions in her online school folder and made this book for her. As Yuki held the book in her lap, she felt embarrassed and pleased but most of all loved. Her mother understood her more than she liked to admit.

"Once upon a time," Yuki read aloud, "deep in the snowy

Siberian forest, lived a tiger named Trudy. Don't forget, you are in the mirror trying to get home."

The reminder jolted Yuki out of her ten-year-old self. In the mirror above the fireplace, she spotted two foamy dots moving toward her. Dread formed in her stomach. Even though she couldn't make out what they were, she had a feeling that the wave snakes were coming for her.

She dropped the book and half ran, half swam away from them. She needed to get to a recent memory of Julio. Instead, she found herself at the zoo. The tiger memory must have led her here. She pushed her way through a sea of brightly colored windbreakers to the railing, where she was suddenly inside her five-year-old self and standing next to Julio. On the other side of the railing, a brown bear played with a ball. They were on a kindergarten field trip. Julio elbowed her. "He's *oso* cute," he said, because *oso* meant "bear" in Spanish. This was the wrong direction. Yuki looked over her shoulder. She could see the wave snakes now, the sea-foam forming horns and fangs.

In a panic, she plowed through the kids along the rail and reentered the tunnel. She looked over her shoulder. The wave snakes were gaining on her. Why had she gone from fifth grade back to kindergarten? What was the connection between the birthday party and the photo book from her mother and the field trip to the zoo? A lion and a tiger and a bear. Lions and tigers and bears. Oh my! The link was *The Wizard of Oz*.

Yuki thought she knew exactly which memory of Julio

she needed. She ran-swam ahead until she saw her house in the Valley decorated for Halloween. Bursting through the front door, she ran to the sofa, where Julio sat reaching into a big bowl of popcorn. They were in seventh grade, too old to go trick-or-treating anymore. On the TV, Dorothy closed her wide, innocent eyes and said, "There's no place like home."

Yuki snapped inside her seventh-grade self, who jumped to her feet and exclaimed, "That's not what she says in the book!"

Julio shushed her.

"I'm serious," Yuki told him. "In the book, Dorothy says, 'Take me home to Aunt Em.'"

Julio threw a handful of popcorn at her and said with frustration, "You say this every year. I don't care what's in the book. Just watch the movie."

His words stung. Yuki slumped down in her seat, her throat feeling tight and raw. Every now and then, Julio made it clear that, like the other kids, he sometimes thought she was an annoying know-it-all. While she wallowed in hurt feelings that matched the bleak Kansas landscape, one wave snake barreled through the fireplace and the other burst through the popcorn bowl.

She looked for a weapon to ward off the snakes. Grabbing the ceramic bowl, she pulled out of her seventh-grade self and crouched on the back of the sofa. She must have made a mistake. Yes, this was the last time she and Julio had watched *The Wizard of Oz* together. But she'd forgotten about the painful moment, about the all-too-true reminder that she sometimes made it hard for her best friend to like her. She loved rules and order because they made her feel safe. But then her father dying had left her feeling very unsafe.

"Hey, maybe next year we can dress up as the flying monkeys," Julio said.

"We're too old to go trick-or-treating, remember?" her seventh-grade self said sulkily.

"But we're not too old to hand out candy," he said.

Tears filled Yuki's eyes. If the wave snakes hadn't come at her right then, she would have hugged Julio. He was the most patient person on the planet, and he deserved a better best friend. One wave snake lunged at her and she bashed its jaw with the bowl. To avoid the shattering pieces, the other wave snake swerved away. Grabbing the knife from her belt, Yuki jumped to the floor and looked for an escape. The wave snake that she had hit listed by the sliding glass door, seemingly stunned. Meanwhile, the other snake made a U-turn at the entryway to the kitchen. Then she saw Julio. Not seventh-grade Julio on the sofa, but present-day Julio— or as close to present-day as she could hope to get—at the end of a tunnel inside the TV screen and holding his COMƎ HOMƎ sign. Once, they had pretended the TV was the portal to Oz. Now it was the way home. The wave snake by the kitchen moved in for another strike. Yuki scrambled through the screen of the TV and ran-swam toward the end of the tunnel, which was clouding over, obscuring Julio. She hoped that didn't mean the portal was closing.

Yuki felt the air around her undulate, which probably

meant the wave snake had entered the passageway. She moved frantically, not daring to look over her shoulder, in case even a split second made the difference between going home and getting chomped. If she made it, she vowed to never complain about PE class again. Every muscle from her eyelids down to her pinkie toes strained forward. She had never pushed herself so hard and moved so slowly. When her body breached the clouded mirror, she shot through with such force that she banged into the wall, the impact knocking a waving cat off the shelf. Leaping to her feet, she turned around to find a wave snake surging toward her. Without thinking, she plunged the knife into the reflection, between the creature's fierce blue eyes. The wave snake froze. Seafoam splattered against the portal, spreading cracks across the surface. And then the mirror shattered.

15

On the Other Side of the Mirror

When Yuki looked down at the floor, she found the mirror had broken into just five large fragments. The knife had disappeared entirely. So had the wave snake. Julio was cowering by the counter, still holding his sign. She could see now that he had tried to write the words backward so that the message would read the right way in the mirror, only he had forgotten to flip the *E*'s. On the other side of the counter, Momo seemed to be having a heated discussion with Hana and Julio's mother, Lupe. Hana and Lupe had on their weekend clothes, jeans and T-shirts, which meant it had to be a Saturday or a Sunday. Momo wore a gold sequined top and looked ready to go to a wedding reception at a stuffy hotel.

"Hi," Yuki said to Julio, her breath coming in quick gasps. She looked down at her clothes. The white blouse and red trouser skirt were gone. She had on her striped T-shirt and jeans, the ones she had left behind in Shōnagon's room.

"Hi," Julio said. "Are you okay? What was that thing?"

"Yuki!" Hana rushed around the counter and clasped her in a tight hug. "You're here," her mother sobbed. "I'm so happy you're here."

Yuki hugged her mother back. "Me, too," she said.

"You said she wasn't here," Lupe said accusingly to Momo.

"I did nothing," Momo said, raising her hands to her chest as if to protect herself. "I told you. I don't like children. Why would I kidnap her?"

"I'm calling the police," Lupe said, pulling her phone out of her purse. "Hana, what was the name of the detective you spoke to?"

"No, Lupe, it's okay," Yuki cried. "It's not Momo's fault. The mirror portal opened and I decided to go."

Yuki assumed that since Julio had been holding up a sign in front of the mirror, Momo must have told them the truth about what had happened—as strange as the truth would sound.

Momo looked frightened as Lupe's curved acrylic fingernail hovered over the keypad of her phone. That's when Yuki realized she hadn't thought once about the impact her disappearing might have on Momo.

"You're saying you went through the mirror like Alice in Wonderland," Hana said. Her mother's face looked puffy from crying.

"Yes," Yuki said. "I know it's hard to believe. But I got to meet Sei Shōnagon and I won a poetry contest at court and I made friends with a talking pheasant. Then it turned out that there was no way to keep the sky from falling, and Regent Fujiwara was pitting everyone against each other. Thankfully, I saw Julio's sign and was able to find my way home."

As her words spilled out, Hana and Lupe exchanged a look of confusion and concern.

"You saw it," Julio said, looking pleased with himself. "I thought if you could see what's her name, the court lady, then you might be able to see the store from the other side."

"Yuki, I'm sure whatever happened to you felt very real," Hana said with a forced calm. "But there's no such thing as a portal that takes you back in time a thousand years."

"I saw Yuki come out," Julio said, pointing to the shards on the floor. "The mirror suddenly turned into a door and Yuki ran through it. This monster was chasing her."

Taking a pencil from Momo's desk, Julio turned over the COMƎ HOMƎ sign and made a rapid sketch of the wave snake. Hana and Lupe exchanged another long, confused look. But Lupe put away her phone.

"I'm sorry that I broke your mirror, Momo," Yuki said, though that was a small thing compared to almost getting Momo arrested.

"It is okay," Momo said. "I am happy you came home."

"How long was I gone?" Yuki asked.

Nobody answered at first. Hana and Lupe both had sharp origami crane faces. Yuki could tell that they thought Julio was covering for her, but they were keeping quiet for now.

"Two days," Momo said. "Today is Saturday."

"Oh, it's our birthday," Yuki said. She was thirteen now. On past birthdays, she'd felt no different. But after all she'd been through in the mirror world, she definitely felt older and wiser. And tired. All Yuki wanted was for her mother to make her a cup of mint tea and then rub her back until she fell asleep.

"Speaking of birthdays, let's get you home," Hana said wearily. "There's still time to celebrate."

"Don't forget your bike," Momo said, pointing to the beach cruiser leaning against the wall.

As Yuki walked her bike toward the door, Momo fell into step with her.

"What was Shōnagon like?" Momo asked in a low whisper. "Did you see the empress? Did you meet other people who came through the mirror?"

"Amazing, yes, and yes," Yuki said. "I'll come by after school sometime this week for tea."

She'd tell Momo all about the contest another time. Right now, she just wanted to go home.

When she walked through the front door, Doug gave her an awkward hug. While he made her some scrambled eggs and toast (she suddenly realized that she was starving), Yuki heard her mother call the police from the living room and explain that her daughter had come home. Did everyone at school know that she had disappeared? She was afraid to ask. That afternoon, Hana, Doug, and Lupe threw together an impromptu birthday party. Doug went out to pick up tempura and tamales ordered from nearby restaurants. Hana and Lupe made a cheese plate and a salad and enlisted Yuki and Julio to bake brownies from a box mix they found in the pantry.

"How did you guys know to come to Momo's store?" Yuki asked in a low voice while Julio held the mixing bowl and she scraped the batter into a pan.

"You left that paper about the court lady's mirror in Momo's store on your desk," Julio said. "Doug knew who she was."

Yuki heard something buzz and Julio fished the flip phone that he never used from his jeans pocket.

"Hey," he said with a wide smile. Yuki could hear a girl's voice on the other end. That had to be Suzie. Julio stepped out to the patio to talk.

On the car ride home, Yuki had imagined Julio apologizing profusely for adding Suzie to their chat and saying what an idiot he'd been for liking someone who would stoop to stealing Pokémon cards out of a friend's backpack. But as he meandered around the patio laughing at something Suzie had said, Yuki knew that wasn't going to happen. And if she wanted Julio to keep being her best friend, she was going to have to be okay with that.

After dinner, Julio handed the sketch of the wave snake to Yuki.

"Happy birthday," he said. "If you send me stories about the mirror world, I'll illustrate them."

"That would be great," Yuki said. She already knew that she would tell her story through lists and poems and moments both big and small.

Then Yuki and Julio bumped fists and fluttered their hands, a move they'd been doing for as long as she could remember.

From her bedroom window, Yuki watched Lupe and Julio drive away. Her old self would have wished she could go with them. But her new self was happy to be in her room again, with her own comfy bed and her books and albums and even the magic mirror. Once, Yuki had asked her father the same question that the scarecrow had asked Dorothy in *The Wonderful Wizard of Oz*. The Land of Oz was filled with color and adventure, while Kansas was boring and gray. Why would Dorothy possibly want to return? Her father had said that home was more about the people we love than the place we lived. Dorothy brought color into Aunt Em's life and Aunt Em loved her. Dorothy loved Aunt Em back. It was that simple. Yuki realized that she'd had the strength to navigate the mirror world because she knew that no matter how far away she traveled or how sassy she had been, her mother would always be waiting for her with open arms.

Once Julio and Lupe turned the corner and she could no longer see their car, Yuki put her father's copy of *The White*

Album on the turntable and logged in to LVLup, where she discovered Julio had invited her to a new chat. When she clicked on the invitation, the screen filled with posts.

Tig1010: Hey, Yu, what's going on??? Your mom just called my mom and said you're missing. They think you ran away. I'm sorry for inviting Troy and Suzie into our chat. I didn't mean to hurt your feelings. Check in if you see this, k?

Tig1010: Hi, it's me again. Please tell me u r hiding in a closet, spying on your mom and Doug. Or maybe camping in a library, kinda like those kids did in the NYC museum in that book we read in fourth grade. If u r, come on out. Srsly, the joke's not funny anymore!

Tig1010: Call me any time if you see this, k? Mama and I are driving to Santa Dolores tomorrow to see your mom and Doug and hang up some flyers, which I know you will hate. You wouldn't want your photo plastered all over lampposts and store windows. Come back so we can celebrate our birthday!

Yuki teared up. She already knew from the vision in the mirror that he cared. But seeing his messages made her realize just how much.

Yuki also had a series of messages from Zoe.

BitterCress: Hey, wassup? You didn't look too good after class yesterday. Miss Ghosh had us diagram this wild sentence in English class.

Yuki couldn't make out the words in the photo that Zoe had uploaded. But the lines branched off and cascaded in downward diagonals. The diagram looked like a car had run over an elaborate wire mobile hanging in an art museum.

BitterCress: Don't tell anyone that I said this because I will call you a liar to your face, but it was actually kinda fun.

BitterCress: If u get bored and wanna play a game, let me know.

BitterCress: Hey, the principal just sent an email asking anyone who had seen you to call????? Hope u r OK.

Yuki leaned back in her chair and swiveled back and forth. Maybe she had been too quick to judge Zoe. Could they be friends? Yuki wasn't sure.

CL4ever: I'm fine. Thanks for asking. I had a fight with my mom and went to visit some friends for a few days.

Then in a Google Doc, Yuki wrote:

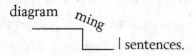

diagram *ming* | sentences.

Emily Dickinson | would have liked |

She took a screenshot and uploaded it to the chat. It was super nerdy. But if Zoe was going to be her friend, she'd have to accept that's who Yuki was.

After logging off, Yuki was tempted to hide in her bed and never go to school again. What was she going to say on Monday when her classmates bombarded her with questions? She had hated feeling invisible at her new school. But imagining them gleefully crowding around her and asking shocked questions was too much. Yuki wondered what Shōnagon would do in her shoes. Shōnagon would own it somehow. She would either say something mysterious or something totally outrageous. What if Yuki said that she'd gone to Japan by herself? That was technically true. And if her classmates asked how she managed to buy an airline ticket and get through passport control, she'd shrug and say, "I have my ways."

Moving to her bed, Yuki listened to the Beatles and shined the flashlight into the mirror on the wall, turning it on, off, on, off, making the lion appear and disappear.

Her mother knocked on the open door. "Can I come in?" she asked.

"Sure," Yuki said.

As Hana slid onto the bed next to her, Yuki took a surreptitious glance at her mother's stomach. But Hana was wearing a loose T-shirt and didn't look noticeably bigger. Hana put her arm around Yuki's shoulders. Yuki leaned into her mother and together they watched the lion appear and disappear on the wall.

"Your father was always quoting from the Alice books," Hana said. "And there's one line that always stayed with me: 'If you'll believe in me, I'll believe in you.'"

"That's what the unicorn says to Alice," Yuki said.

"I was thinking we could try that," Hana said.

Yuki nodded. "That sounds fabulous, Monster," she said.

"Okay, good," Hana said. "You know, I think I like this magic mirror."

"Yeah, me, too," Yuki said as she switched the flashlight on, off, on, off.

"I was also thinking maybe we could restart pizza and movie night, only it doesn't have to be pizza and a movie," Hana said. "Just the two of us spending time together. We could get our nails done and go out for bubble tea."

"I'd like that," Yuki said. "Mom, are you—are you going to have a baby?"

Her mother gasped and hugged Yuki tighter. "Oh, Yuki," Hana said. "I was going to give you the night to settle in and tell you tomorrow. How did you know?"

"I saw your test in the trash," Yuki said.

Hana brought her hand to her mouth and was quiet for a shocked second. "I'm so sorry you had to find out that way," she said.

Yuki shrugged and clicked the flashlight on, off, on, off. "It's okay," she said.

"This kid is going to worship you, you know," Hana said. "And you're not going to believe how much love you're going to feel. I also want you to know that there will always be enough love to go around in this family, and when I say family, that includes your father. He will always be part of us."

"Yeah, I know that now," Yuki said. "We'll have to find the box with all my old picture books. I can read *Moo, Baa, La La La!* to the baby."

Her mother kissed her on the forehead. "I think the baby will love that," she said.

As they watched the lion appear and disappear on the

wall and listened to the guitar gently weep, Doug passed by the bedroom door and stopped.

"Oh, there you are," Doug said. "Sorry, I didn't mean to interrupt. I just wanted to say good night. I'm going to bed."

As he turned to go, Yuki called out, "Hey, Doug. Thanks for the magic mirror. I really love it."

Doug put his hands in his pockets and raised his shoulders in a modest shrug. "I'm glad you like it, Yuki, and I'm glad you're home," he said. "Now I just have to get you to laugh at one of my jokes."

"Actually, I have one that you might like," Yuki said. "A samurai hops into the bar. His left arm and his left leg have been cut clean off. The bartender says, 'You must have been in a terrible duel,' and the samurai says, 'Oh, I'm all right.'"

Doug looked startled. Then, as her words sank in, an appreciative grin spread across his face. "He's all right," Doug said. "That's a good one."

That night, Yuki dreamed she was in an old Japanese house that creaked with the wind. The floors were splintered. The shutters were weather-beaten. The blinds were worn and shabby. Through the heavy mist, she could just make out a stone lantern and the branches of a tree in the garden.

When she turned around, the eight priestesses were folding paper flowers while Shōnagon and Murasaki arranged the bright blooms in vases. Nobu was offering a bowl of berries to the pheasant. And Izumi was grinding an ink stick against the ink stone. When she finished making the ink, she pushed a stack of thick, creamy paper toward Yuki.

"What should we write about?" Izumi asked.

"Things that are especially delightful," Yuki said. "I'll start."

Sources

I first encountered *The Pillow Book* by Sei Shōnagon in a Japanese literature course during my junior year abroad in Tokyo. A book written at the turn of the eleventh century by a lady-in-waiting at the imperial court sounded like a slog. Yet from the very first page, I was captivated by her breezy, vibrant account of her life at court and, of course, by her lists. While the quality of the prose cannot be compared, it struck me that the letters my best friend Shannon and I wrote chronicling the funny exchanges, dramas, and fashions at our middle school—often interspersed with parody song lyrics—were in the same spirit as *The Pillow Book*. I've always wanted to create a fictional character based on Shōnagon. So when I dreamed up the idea of a middle schooler finding a portal to an alternate dimension modeled on Heian-era Japan, I finally had my chance.

Since this is a fantasy world, I've taken a historical liberty and put Shōnagon at court with Murasaki Shikibu, author of

The Tale of Genji. While these two literary giants did serve rival empresses (Shōshi was eventually elevated to empress), their service at court did not overlap. A quick note on names: *Shōnagon* refers to her title, minor counselor, which is how everyone addresses her in the Ivan Morris translation of *The Pillow Book. Sei* comes from the first character in her family name, Kiyohara. Her first name is believed to be Nagiko. Murasaki Shikibu's name is unknown. *Shikibu* is also a title, and she later became known as Murasaki after the character in her book.

For period details, I relied on *The World of the Shining Prince: Court Life in Ancient Japan* by Ivan Morris; *The Cambridge History of Japan, Volume 2: Heian Japan*, edited by Donald H. Shively and William H. McCullough; and the Costume Museum in Kyoto.

For diagramming sentences, I turned to the wonderful *Sister Bernadette's Barking Dog: The Quirky History and Lost Art of Diagramming Sentences* by Kitty Burns Florey. Any diagramming mistakes are my own.

The wave snake (*namija*) and the enchanted paper lantern (*chōchin obake*) are two of many fantastical creatures from Japanese folklore. You can learn more about them on http://yokai.com, written and illustrated by Matthew Meyer.

Acknowledgments

When I sat down to write my debut novel, *The Pearl Hunter*, the COVID-19 pandemic had just shut down New York City. Other than taking neighborhood walks and binge-ing *Gilmore Girls* and playing an epic game of rummy 500 with my family, I had very little else to fill my days. Writing fiction became a welcome distraction during that dull and unsettling time.

I wrote *Through a Clouded Mirror* under completely differ-ent circumstances. Life had come roaring back with myriad demands that could not be put off or ignored. It's much eas-ier, it turns out, to write amid the quiet than amid the noise. I never would have found my way to Yuki's story without the guidance and support of my agent, Victoria Wells Arms, and my editor, Donna Bray. I'm also grateful to Beth Ain and Leila Mohr for their generous feedback and friendship.

And finally, thanks to Howard and Talia for their love and support. As long as we're together, wherever we are in time and space is home.